"You want me to be honest with you?"

"Yes."

Her expression exuded hurt. "Then no," she told him, her lower lip suddenly quavering as much as the rest of her, "I don't think you desire me. And since the *last* thing that I want right now, Doc, after being pressured into accepting a fixed-up date, is a *pity* kiss..."

That was it. Jack had heard enough. Doing what he had wanted to do from the first moment he had laid eyes on her this evening, he wrapped his arms around her, brought her close enough to feel the wild, erratic beating of her heart.

"Damn it, Bess. Don't you get it? Pity is the last thing I'm feeling..." He lowered his face to hers, fastened his lips over hers. Admitting softly, penitently, "Regret maybe, for waiting this long..."

Dear Reader,

Christmas is not just a time of joy, it's also a time to reflect, and Bess Monroe is in a funk. Everyone else in her family is married with kids and living the life she dreams about. Unfortunately, the closest she can get to familial happiness is in the time she spends with widower Jack McCabe and his three adorable little girls. So when pressed to write an annual Christmas letter, she instead writes two—one ridiculously happy, one ridiculously glum. Neither is ever supposed to be seen! But you know what they say about life—it's what happens when you are making other plans...

Jack appreciates Bess, and the help she has given him, more than he could ever say. Most of all, he wants Bess to be happy and to have everything she yearns for. When he gets wind of her two holiday letters, he rushes to her aid, determined to help her the way she has always helped him. The surprise? He may have to set aside their agreement, to be only friends, to make this their best Christmas ever!

I hope you all have a wonderful holiday!

Happy reading!

Cathy Gillen Thacker

CathyGillenThacker.com

A Tale of Two Christmas Letters

Cathy Gillen Thacker

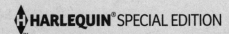

H HARLEQUIN®SPECIAL EDITION

Recycling programs
for this product may
not exist in your area.

ISBN-13: 978-1-335-57428-2

ISBN-13: 978-1-335-57428-2

A Tale of Two Christmas Letters

Copyright © 2019 by Cathy Gillen Thacker

Printed in U.S.A.

Cathy Gillen Thacker is married and a mother of three. Her mysteries, romantic comedies and heartwarming family stories have made numerous appearances on bestseller lists, but her best reward, she says, is knowing one of her books made someone's day a little brighter. She loves telling passionate stories with happy endings and thinks nothing beats a good romance and a hot cup of tea! You can visit Cathy's website, cathygillenthacker.com, for more information on her books, recipes, and a list of her favorite things.

Books by Cathy Gillen Thacker

Harlequin Special Edition

Texas Legends: The McCabes

The Texas Cowboy's Quadruplets
His Baby Bargain
Their Inherited Triplets

Harlequin Western Romance

Texas Legends: The McCabes

The Texas Cowboy's Triplets
The Texas Cowboy's Baby Rescue

Texas Legacies: The Lockharts

A Texas Soldier's Family
A Texas Cowboy's Christmas
The Texas Valentine Twins
Wanted: Texas Daddy
A Texas Soldier's Christmas

Visit the Author Profile page
at Harlequin.com for more titles.

Chapter One

"Ho, ho, ho, and merry Christmas," the low, sexy male voice murmured from the open doorway.

Bess Monroe looked up and saw Jack McCabe standing in the portal of her minuscule office, holding what looked to be a horrendously familiar piece of paper in his hand. As usual, on his surgery days, blue hospital scrubs cloaked his big, buff frame. A matching blue cap covered his cropped dark brown hair, and a mischievous grin tugged at the corners of his lips.

"Or should I say," her longtime friend teased, bringing out a second page from behind his back, "bah humbug?"

Bess moaned and went back to hiding her face in her hands. This had to be one of the worst days of her life. Her humiliation increasing by leaps and bounds, she pleaded, "Go away."

"Not until I hear the undoubtedly fascinating full

story behind these two missives," Jack said, stepping inside, shutting the door behind him and closing the distance between them in two laconic strides.

Bess pursed her lips in exasperation as he proceeded to sit on the side of her desk, his long legs stretched out in front of him.

"Hey," he said, touching her shoulder and inundating her with his clean, manly scent, "you know you can talk to me."

That was the problem, she thought, close enough to feel the heat emanating from him.

She could.

And she couldn't.

With a sigh, she lifted her head, letting her gaze shift over him. At six feet four inches tall, with broad shoulders and a fit, athletic body, he had an admirable ability to exude both the top-notch confidence of an excellent orthopedic surgeon and the innate compassion of a natural-born healer.

He had also never come close to humiliating himself the way she just had.

She pushed her chair all the way back and stood. "What do you want me to say?" She spread her hands wide. "My legendary tech skills get better by the day."

Briefly, he seemed confused. He watched her move about the small space restlessly. "Okay, enough dodging. Are you going to tell me what happened or not?"

Figuring she might as well confess her sins to someone, she huffed out a breath. "You know how my nursing school graduating class has a tradition of sending out annual Christmas letters to each other?"

The corners of his lips curved up sympathetically. "I recall it's never been your favorite thing."

Mostly because it seemed like everyone else had

everything *she* wanted. And it was getting increasingly difficult to deal with how far away she was from achieving any of her life goals except those regarding her career. Especially now that she was thirty-two... and getting older by the minute.

"Can you blame me?" Bess shrugged. "Given the fact I generally don't have anything really worthwhile to report on the personal level. At least not to the level everyone else does." With their gorgeous husbands, kids, pets, homes, she thought a little jealously.

Jack nodded, understanding. Life had given him unexpected heartache, too. Heartache that, three years later, she knew he was still dealing with.

Aware the combination of nerves and stress was making her knees a little wobbly, she went back to her chair and sat down. "So, in order to give myself a break, I planned on skipping the written update altogether this year." If only she had followed her instincts and done that! "But my twin, Bridgett, wouldn't let it go. And she kept bugging me to get on it."

Recognition gleamed in Jack's cobalt blue eyes. He rubbed a hand over the beginnings of a five o'clock shadow on his chiseled jaw. "So you wrote two instead of just one?"

Bess winced, tingling everywhere his gaze had touched, as well as everywhere it hadn't. "Um. Not intentionally."

Again, he waited.

She gulped. "The first one...the Grinchy one...was written as sort of a way of thumbing my nose at the whole process."

"And the second, extraordinarily cheery one?"

"Was written just as tongue in cheek," she answered. "I actually didn't intend to send either one of them. I left them both as drafts and forgot about them, figuring I would go back to the task when I was in a better mood." Which she'd figured would be never.

"And then?"

She flushed. "The next time I went to open up my email, the draft file somehow got emptied, too, and both letters were accidentally sent to all my nursing school pals. Everyone thought it was a joke and couldn't wait to share them. And now…well, even you've heard about that colossal mistake."

"Everyone in the hospital has."

Which was probably what she deserved for being such a smart aleck. And envious, to boot. When she knew darn well she shouldn't be. After all, she had plenty to be happy about. Even if she didn't have the husband or the children she had always wanted.

Figuring their intimate exchange had gone on long enough, she moved slowly to her feet once again. "Guess the joke is on me."

Jack stood, too. "Except it wasn't really a joke, was it?" he guessed with his trademark kindness. "That's genuinely how you feel."

Jack hadn't come in here to make Bess feel worse. He'd intended to rescue her from whatever this was, the way she had rescued him and his three little girls so many times since his wife had died. But now that he was here, he saw she was in real trouble. Even if she didn't want anyone to know how much.

Bess blushed. She stepped around him toward the door. "I don't know what you're talking about."

Figuring if someone had to confront her, it may as well be him, Jack eased behind her desk and took her chair. "No problem," he countered cheerfully. "I can refresh your memory easily enough." Waggling his brows at her, he shook out the first letter and read out loud:

"'Dear friends and fellow nurses, what an incredibly sucky year this has been. The transmission on my beloved Volvo sedan died a week after the warranty expired. (You don't want to know how many thousands of dollars it took to replace it.) Then I bought the house I've always wanted, only to have it turn into a total money pit, too. I've spent way too much on contractors and supplies, and a zillion hours working on it, and I still haven't finished painting the interior! Which needs to be done before I bring my new puppy home. Because once that happens, I know I'll have zero time to do anything house-related. At least for the first year or so.'"

Jack looked at her, taking in her slender five-foot-seven-inch frame, glossy brown hair and soft pink lips. Maybe it was because she was smaller and so much more delicately built than him, but he always felt the need to protect her. At first, kind of like a cousin or a little sis. Now it was something...different.

He wondered if she had any idea how vulnerable and pretty she looked standing there in the late-afternoon November sunlight streaming through the hospital windows. Or how many men in Laramie County wanted to go after her, and would if they thought they'd have any hope of success.

But that wasn't happening. Not with that barbed wire barrier she kept around her heart.

Working to keep his own feelings in check, he looked down at her. "You know you could ask for help with the house."

"It's my problem. I'll handle it."

That was just it, Jack thought, his gaze once again running over the taut, supple body encased in the black cotton scrubs the hospital's rehabilitation staff wore. She didn't have to handle any of this herself, not when he was standing by, but he would discuss that with her later.

He resumed reading.

"'Of course, it's probably good I'll be so busy and have a precious pet to love…and love me back…since the man I'm wildly in love with is in love with someone else and always will be.'"

Jack paused. Aware for reasons he couldn't quite understand that this part of her confession had really thrown him for a loop. Maybe because he'd never noticed her lusting after anyone in their orbit. He looked at her over the top of the paper, acutely aware it wasn't like the oh-so-sweet and incredibly practical Bess to chase after lost causes. "Care to identify the object of your affection?" he asked mildly.

"No."

He caught the spark of temper in her dark green eyes. "Okay. Moving on." Her mouth was kind of pouty, too. "Where were we? Oh, yeah." He read on, "'Sadly, as excited as I am to be getting a golden retriever, I haven't had a decent date in forever and hence am no closer to getting married and/or having kids.'"

Which would be a shame, he thought sympathetically. He knew from the way Bess interacted with his own daughters that she would be a great mother.

He cleared his throat, aware the next passage seemed even more unlike the coworker he thought he knew. "'So, it looks as if I'll spend the rest of my life, not to mention every Christmas from here on out, as the eternally single aunt and good friend who is lucky enough to have a gorgeous, wonderful dog but is also hopelessly, permanently unattached. And that, dear friends, is all I've got to report. Sourly yours, Dess Monroe.'"

Jack put the paper aside. "Wow. Pretty dark, Nurse Bess. Except for the stuff about the puppy."

Bess folded her arms, her expression defiant. "I wrote another one," she pointed out with exaggerated pleasantness.

Appreciating the fire in her eyes, Jack turned to that missive. "I liked that email, too." He made a great show of holding it up. "'Dear friends and family,'" he began to read aloud.

She covered her ears and moaned again in a way that had his heart rate accelerating. "Please don't."

Undeterred, Jack continued, "'I am ever so pleased to report that this has been the year of my dreams. My beloved Volvo sedan is not only completely paid off now, but running better than ever, thanks to the brand-new transmission I put into it! The shotgun house I bought gets more charming and cozy by the day. And all the hands-on work I've done has left me incredibly fit and lithe.'"

Jack paused. "Have to agree with you there, pal."

Another beat of silence fell. She made a face. "I can't believe you just said that."

He shrugged, glad to see some of her usual sass coming back. "What are friends for, if not to compliment you?"

She lifted a censuring brow, suggesting none-too-kindly, "They could be quiet."

He chuckled.

He knew what she wanted. To pretend this had never happened. That he, and everyone else in her world, had never had a glimpse into her wounded soul.

What *he* really wanted was to see her smile the way

she did when she was really and truly happy. To hear her laugh again. Which, come to think of it, hadn't been for a while now, he realized, disturbed by the revelation.

Frowning, he tore his gaze from the mesmerizing depths of her dark green eyes and returned his attention to the printed page. "Hmm. Where were we?"

Bess harrumphed with Scroogey finesse. "Done," she said.

No. They weren't. And they wouldn't be until she admitted what was really going on with her.

"Ah, yes, here we are," he said, smugly reciting from her letter. "'Which is great, because there's no better time to be down an entire dress size than when you're crazy in love with the man of your dreams, and he feels the same way about you…'"

Again with the object of her affection. Jack looked up, feeling a tinge of emotion he chose not to identify. "Do I know this guy?" he asked suspiciously. He couldn't help wondering about the guy who seemed to be breaking Bess's spirit, not to mention her heart.

She glared at him.

"'Cause I'd like to meet him," Jack added before he could stop himself.

Bess released a mirthless laugh. "No way we're going down that road, pardner."

Not sure if her refusal to fess up the identity of her secret crush made him happy or sad, Jack continued reading from her letter. "'…and hope to one day soon have a family together.'"

He paused, feeling an unexpected surge of jealousy. "I really do need to meet this guy," he muttered. Especially if this fella was making her so unhappy.

"I have two brothers who can do the potential screening, thanks."

Nick and Gavin Monroe were protective of family, but would they be as discerning as Jack would be in vetting Bess's potential boyfriends? He thought not.

Scowling, he went back to reading the last of her letter. "'So, along with the gorgeous little golden retriever puppy I will soon bring home, I will therefore spend every year…from here on out…with the man of my dreams…living out all my wildest fantasies…'"

Jack realized he would like to know what those fantasies were, too. Not that he should be letting his imagination go there.

He cleared his throat. "'So merry Christmas, everyone! I hope you all have had the absolutely incredible twelve months I have. Cheerfully yours, Bess Monroe.'"

Jack set the letter down, on top of the first. "That's definitely a better ending." Although he wasn't sure he bought either version. Never mind the parts about her secret love.

Wouldn't he have known if she'd been seeing someone? Especially given how much time she spent with him and his girls on the weekends? Just hanging out, and filling in when Mrs. D. was either off duty or away?

Bess snatched the pages from his hands. "I hope you feel better now. Because I sure don't!" she fumed.

"Hey," he said softly. "I wasn't trying to upset you."

"Then what was the point of that humiliating recitation?" She slapped the papers in her desk drawer and slammed it shut, appearing ready to both scream in outrage and burst into sobs simultaneously.

Guilt flowed through him. "The point was to get you to talk to me." He rose, crossed the distance between them and put his hands on her shoulders. "And let me know how I can help," he countered, able to see how badly she needed comforting. Even if touching each other wasn't something they usually did.

Except by accident.

Tensing, she buried her face in her hands. "You can't," she choked out, sounding even more miserable. "No one can."

"I don't believe that," he said quietly. Then his next idea hit. "Do you want me to talk to this guy...whoever he is?"

"Absolutely not!" she replied, horrified, stiffening all the more.

She had helped him out so much over the past few years, he knew he owed her. "Sure?" he persisted, reluctantly letting go of her and stepping back.

Bess composed herself with her usual grace. "Yes. What I feel... Let's just say it's destined to be an unrequited love."

He gave her another reassuring touch on her forearm. "You're certain?"

Bess's chin trembled. "Yes." She swallowed. "I just need to get over it. Find a way to move on. Which, in all honesty, is the real reason I wrote those letters. So I would get it all out and see how foolish I'm being, even thinking about him, when I know there's no real interest on the other side, at least not the kind I want and need," she concluded, matter-of-fact.

Jack understood wishing for the impossible, as well as the comfort that could be gleaned from a close and lasting friendship. The kind he wished they had, because up to now, it had been mostly one of utility, centered around the needs of his kids, rather than their own.

Aware this was the first time she'd let him in, he did the same for her, confessing quietly, "The holidays are hard for me, too." There were times when he was overcome with grief. And guilt…

Her slender shoulders relaxed, ever so slightly. "I know."

He frowned, thinking about his late wife. It had been three years since she died, but it felt like forever. "I miss Gayle." *And feel desperately lonely. Ready to move on.* "I worry I'm not doing enough for the girls."

Her breath hitching, Bess lifted her gaze to his. Their shared sorrow shone in her eyes. Acceptance, too. She regarded him fiercely. "You do plenty for Lindsay, Nicole and Chloe, Jack."

He sure as hell tried. It wasn't enough.

And never would be.

"Except I can't bring their mother back," he said tersely. "So every year for me, I feel like I'm Charlie Brown at Christmastime."

"Privately depressed," she guessed. "Even though you know that, given everything you do still have, you should be happy."

"Right."

Bess reached over and covered his hand with hers. "I never realized that you were feeling that way."

With a rueful smile, he looked down at their casually linked fingers. "I put on a good show. I have to. Otherwise, the entire McCabe clan would descend on me in force."

Understanding lit her eyes. "Same here with the Monroes."

"And I don't want to let my daughters down. They deserve to have the best Christmas possible. Despite not having a mom around to enjoy it with us."

She paused as if to weigh their situations. Then brought

him close for a warm, companionable hug. "I'm sorry if my pity party brought you down."

He gave her a supportive squeeze, too. "You didn't." They stepped back. "We're pals. Pals help each other out. And that being the case…" He looked her in the eye, not bothering to disguise his hope she would rush to his aid once again.

She shook her head, her mood turning wry. "You really have something else to ask me, Doc? After all those really nosy questions?"

The kind they had never asked each other before this. In fact, it was their mutual lack of prying and giving each other plenty of emotional space while still spending time together that had helped them stay friends since his wife had died. They'd kept up the same pattern later when Bess's engagement had ended.

But now that he was here…why not solve two problems at once? Ease Bess's melancholy and solve his much thornier problem?

He grinned and asked, "Want to have dinner with me and the girls tonight?"

Chapter Two

Bess looked at the handsome physician still standing opposite her. "I assume by the way you just said that there's an ulterior motive?"

He lifted his hands. "I need you to talk them out of something."

Of course he did. His three little girls were known for both their stubbornness and their indefatigable efforts to always get their own way. Fortunately, Jack's fifty-six-year-old housekeeper and nanny was pretty good at getting and keeping them on track. "Can't Mrs. Deaver back you up?"

Jack scrubbed a hand across his face. "She'd prefer not to get involved with this one."

Bess paused, aware that the mystery of whatever was going on in his estrogen-fueled household had already drawn her in. Even though she knew she had to be careful not to get too involved in the sexy widower's problems, given her current emotionally vulnerable state.

"Which begs the question, then, Doc. Should I?" she retorted, enjoying the switch back to their usual playful banter.

The corners of Jack's eyes crinkled. "Just join us for pizza."

As she had many times in the past when he required an extra hand corralling his girls. She sighed. Why was he so damned hard to resist? And why did he keep coming back to her for help, when he could have had any number of other single females in the community rushing to his aid?

Oh, that was right. He picked her because he'd never been attracted to her. And assumed—wrongly, as it happened—she felt exactly the same about him.

As if sensing she was on the edge of refusing, Jack took her hand and said, "Please?"

Her hand tingling, Bess stepped away from him and moved behind her desk to power down her computer. "All right," she said, pretending the absolute last thing she wanted was to spend time with him. She grabbed her coat and bag. "You've convinced me."

The corners of his lips lifted in a brilliant smile. "The girls will be so pleased."

But what about you, Jack? How do you feel? Am I just a convenience? A family friend? Backup nanny or mother figure? And if that's all I am, how much longer can I go on this way?

He walked her out into the hallway, his nearness inundating her with the smell of wintergreen breath mints, hospital soap and the brisk masculine essence that was him. "Six thirty okay?"

Bess nodded. "I've got to go home and change clothes, but then I'll be over," she said as they reached the elevators in the hospital annex where all the offices were located. As she turned to look up at him, she couldn't help but think about how much taller he was, and she wondered what it would feel like to be hauled up against his hard, strong body and kissed. "I can't stay too long, though. I've got to visit my new puppy tomorrow." She was really holding on to that ray of sunshine in her life. She needed that kind of boundless love.

"Well, what do you know?" Jack said, feigning astonishment. "I've got an appointment with Winfield Golden Retrievers, too."

She knew he'd been thinking about putting a deposit down on one of the female pups in the litter because he'd asked her a gazillion questions. About dogs in general, which were good for kids, this particular type of sporting dog and, most important of all, the breeder.

Bess set down her bag and struggled into her jacket. When it got caught around her midriff, he reached over to help her. Tamping down the pleasure the mere brush of his fingertips evoked, she tugged the ends of her long hair from her collar and asked, "Do the girls know?"

"No." Ever chivalrous, he picked up her bag and handed it to her. "I'm hoping to surprise them with the news tomorrow. If their first meet and greet at the ranch where you're getting your new puppy goes well, that is."

"It will," Bess promised. His children had wanted a pet for as long as she had, especially four-year-old Nicole.

"Let's hope so," Jack said as the doors slid open.

As their eyes met, Bess had the oddest sensation he wanted to say or do something else. But the moment passed. Instead, he simply reached out and stopped the elevator doors from closing, holding them for her. With a smile of thanks, she stepped inside. And that, it seemed, was that.

* * *

What had he been thinking? Jack chastised himself as the elevator doors closed and he headed off in the opposite direction. He had almost reached out to hug her goodbye. Or maybe walk her all the way to her car.

He and Bess did not escort each other to their vehicles. They did not hug hello and goodbye. Or discuss intimate personal issues. Or, God forbid, feelings. They were good "family friends" who helped each other out.

Yes, he'd broken protocol just now, when they were still in her office, and she was so distraught.

But normally, Bess made it clear she liked her physical space…at least when it came to him…and didn't want him invading it.

Message received. Not exactly wanted, but always received.

He supposed it was the season making him acutely aware of his own loneliness. Making him want what he could not have. Jack released a weary sigh. Like it or not, Bess wasn't the only one exceedingly vulnerable this year.

"Daddy!" Jack's three little girls squealed in delight an hour later. "Bess is here!" Oblivious of the cold November air, they opened their front door wide and ushered her inside their large Victorian home.

"Hi, girls!" Bess knelt to hug them all in turn and receive their wildly enthusiastic embraces. "I hear we're having pizza tonight."

All had their late mom's blond curls and turquoise eyes. Lindsay, age six, was clad in her usual pastel jeans, sparkly T-shirt and matching sneakers. Four-year-old Nicole wore a ruffled dress, tights and ballet slippers. Three-year-old Chloe wore a sweater with a teddy bear appliqué on the front, warm leggings and cowgirl boots.

All three talked at once.

"Hi, Bess! Are you excited 'bout Christmas? Daddy says we can't always have everything we want."

Wasn't that the truth, Bess thought, sighing inwardly.

Jack strolled up to join them. He'd changed into khakis and a long-sleeved olive green polo shirt. He took Bess's jacket. "Slow down, ladies. Give her a chance to catch her breath."

Mrs. D. came into the hallway. Her salt-and-pepper hair was swept back into a sleek knot at the nape of her neck. She had a wool coat on over her tailored slacks and sweater, and a bag slung over her shoulder. "Hi, Bess."

Bess greeted the woman fondly. She had worked for Jack since his wife died. She lived nearby and was on her own most weekends. She stayed with the family Monday morning through Friday evening, and whenever Jack was on call for the hospital or had other obligations that required him to have an adult at home. "Headed out?" Bess asked.

Mrs. D. nodded, then turned to Jack. "If you need me, you know where to find me. Otherwise, I'll see you all first thing Monday morning."

Jack grinned. "Thanks, Mrs. D." Once the door shut behind the housekeeper, he motioned for Bess and the girls to follow him to the back of the house. "The pizza just arrived."

They all sat down at the table. Bess had been there so many times it was like a second home to her. "So what's going on?" she asked the kids, once again putting her secret attraction to Jack aside.

"We want to write our letters to Santa, but Daddy says it's not time yet," Nicole explained.

Jack gave Bess a look that let her know this was what he needed help with. "It's not even Thanksgiving yet," he reminded the girls.

"It will be next week!" Chloe said. "And we always get our tree right after that!"

Bess recalled how important the holiday had been to Gayle. He had continued their traditions, for the girls.

"So we could mail our letters then, if they were all done," Lindsay said.

Bess noted that Jack was looking awfully tense. She helped herself to some of the salad Mrs. Deaver had left for them. "Do you girls know what you want to ask for?"

Lindsay nodded. "I want him to come to our house this year and leave our presents here, not at Grandma and Grandpa's house."

Now Jack looked really stressed.

"I want a puppy," Nicole announced, "like the one you're going to get, Bess. Only I want Santa to bring it down the chimney."

Which explained Jack's urgency to have the girls meet the puppies in the litter and see how they reacted to each other.

"I want a new baby," Chloe said sweetly. "A real one."

"Santa doesn't bring real babies," Lindsay huffed.

"He will, too, if you ask nicely!" Chloe argued.

Bess began to see why Jack had called for reinforcement. "You know," she intervened, aware this was a really uncomfortable topic for Jack, given the tragedy that had happened the last time a baby arrived in his family, "I think Santa brings baby dolls to little girls."

"But he brings puppies. I know he does," Nicole said, "because my friends got puppies last year."

"Well, I don't care what Santa brings as long as he

comes to our house this year and brings it down *our* chimney," Lindsay pouted.

"Actually," Jack said casually, "I have it on pretty good authority that Santa was planning on leaving your presents at Grandma and Grandpa's ranch house again this year."

Lindsay's lower lip shot out. "I want him to come here," she stated.

Jack sent Bess a helpless look.

She dived in to find out the reason behind his eldest daughter's defiant request. "Why is it so important Santa come here instead of somewhere else?" she asked.

Lindsay picked the cheese off her pizza. "Because he comes to all my friends' houses."

Nicole nodded. "I think he should come here, too."

Chloe stuck her thumb in her mouth. "Me, too."

"Sounds like you're outnumbered," Bess told Jack when the meal had concluded and the girls ran upstairs to get their pajamas on.

"I was hoping that, unlike my parents…and Mrs. D., you'd take my side on this," he grumbled.

"I wish I could," Bess said, determined not to put herself in an emotionally vulnerable situation with him.

"But…?"

She held his gaze. Struggled not to notice how good he looked and smelled, like bergamot and suede. She moved her eyes on the strong column of his throat and the tufts of dark brown hair visible in the open collar of his shirt. When she felt composed enough, she returned her gaze to his. "They want normal, Jack. And what normal means to them this year is celebrating in their own home. But that doesn't mean you have to go it entirely on your own."

"Mrs. D. spends Christmas with her daughter and

her family every year. It would be unfair of me to ask her to come in, even for a little bit, even though I know she'd probably do it out of pity."

She wondered how he could look so cool and confident when she felt so emotionally frazzled just discussing this. "That doesn't mean you can't invite your folks to come here for Christmas Eve and Christmas morning."

"First of all…" Jack rubbed his hand across his closely shaved jaw. "…they're hosting a big McCabe family get-together on their ranch on Christmas Eve, and another brunch for friends who don't have family nearby on Christmas morning, so it's not practical to ask them to do that. Second…" Sadness filled his eyes. "…it reminds me…"

Her heart clutched. "Of Gayle," she said, resisting the urge to take him in her arms and hold him until their mutual sorrow faded. She had known and loved his late wife, an ob-gyn at the hospital, too… She swallowed hard around the lump in her throat. "Everyone who knew her misses her, too," she murmured when she could speak again.

Broad shoulders taut with tension, Jack turned away. Slid the leftover pizza into the fridge. When he appeared to get his emotions under control, he turned back to her, his posture casual as ever. "I don't want to be sad."

She adapted an equally nonchalant stance. It was time both of them moved on. Likely in different directions. "Maybe you won't be."

He studied her, as if trying to decide how much further he wanted this discussion to go.

She squirmed under his scrutiny. It was disconcerting, as a single woman with no children of her own, giving this father of three parenting advice. "Look. The girls feel the way they feel. You can either argue with them about this for the next month, or suck it up and give them what they all really seem to need."

An indefinable emotion flickered in his eyes. The corners of his lips slanted downward. "Is this your version of tough love?"

"All I can tell you is that when I lost my parents in that car accident when I was sixteen, holidays were hard. But my siblings and I survived them by staying at the ranch and celebrating all the holiday traditions our folks held dear."

He rubbed the tense muscles at the back of his neck. Exhaled. "Okay, so assume I give in on this point, and the puppy—"

"Which should prove a monumental distraction."

"—there's still the matter of the new baby to address."

Bess shook her head and lifted both hands in surrender. "You're on your own with that one, Doc."

Because, truth to tell, she was aching for a baby, too.

Bess wasn't quite sure how he'd managed it, but by the time she'd been on her way out his door last night, Jack had somehow managed to convince her to ride with them to the Winfield Golden Retrievers ranch the next morning.

As usual, the girls were full of questions for her.

"Why do you want a puppy?"

"So I won't have to be so lonely," Bess said before she could think.

Jack slanted her a look from behind the wheel.

Self-conscious, she tried again. "What I mean by that is, if I have a dog, then I won't have to come home to an empty house at the end of the day."

That sounded even worse. Like she didn't have any friends. Or family. And she had plenty of both.

Fortunately, Jack seemed to understand what she was trying to say. "You can never underestimate the value of a good companion, girls. Which is why we all like having Bess spend so much time with us. Because she's great company. Right?"

"Yes! She's the best! We love Bess!"

Bess flushed. She knew Jack's girls loved her as much as she loved them. Which made her predicament all the worse. She had to stop privately lusting after their father.

Luckily, more questions followed.

"Do you want a girl doggy or a boy doggy?"

Bess replied, "A girl dog, definitely."

"What do you think, Daddy? What kind of doggy is best?"

"I think they're all great," Jack said diplomatically.

A sentiment that was driven home when they arrived at the ranch and entered the carpeted, sunlit room where the litter of four-week-old golden retriever puppies and their mama were housed. A whelping pen stood in one corner. The door was open and the mama lay on her side inside the pen.

"As you can see, we've got six females and three males," Betty Winfield said. "They're approximately four to five pounds each right now."

Giggling, the girls watched the puppies rollick across the floor, tumbling and leaping over each other, taking turns with the assortment of puppy toys scattered about. "Can we pet them?" Nicole asked, enthralled.

"Absolutely," Betty said.

Chloe beamed. "They are so cuuuute, Daddy!"

Yes, Bess thought, they were. In fact, the fluffy,

golden-haired little pups were so adorable, she was going to have a hard time choosing which one to take home with her in three weeks. She placed her bag on the table next to the door and sank down on the middle of the carpet.

"How come there are colored dots on their backs?" Lindsay asked.

"That's so we can tell them apart," Betty said. "Each puppy has a different color and we call them by that name right now."

"Green likes me!" Nicole said.

"Red likes Bess," Chloe noted, cuddling close to Bess and the puppy that had climbed onto her lap.

"Pet them, Daddy!" Lindsay urged.

Jack sat down, cross-legged on the floor, next to his daughters. For the next half hour, they all had a chance to get acquainted with all nine puppies. But Red kept coming back to Bess, and Green stayed with Nicole.

Smiling, Jack finally asked, "Girls, what would you think about getting a puppy here, too?"

Nicole frowned like he'd just made the worst suggestion ever. "No, Daddy!"

He blinked in confusion. "No?"

"Santa Claus is bringing my puppy to me," Nicole huffed.

"Yeah, down the chimney at our house!" Lindsay said.

"On Christmas morning," Chloe clarified. "With the new baby brother."

Now it was a brother, and not just a baby? Bess thought, wincing inwardly. The yuletide dreams continued.

Betty lifted a brow at Jack. "You're having a new baby, too?"

"No!" Briefly, Jack looked like that was the last thing

he'd ever wanted. "We're talking about baby dolls," he explained.

"Uh-uh," Chloe protested. "I want a real baby brother, a little brother, like my friend Darcy has."

"Jack's girls have been talking a lot about what they want to ask Santa for this year," Bess explained.

Betty caught on. She smiled and let the subject drop, going back to the real reason why they were all here. "You still get first pick," she told Bess. "So if you've made a decision…?"

Bess didn't have to think twice. She looked down at the adorable little puppy curled up in her lap, fast asleep. They had bonded from the moment they'd met. "Red," she said. "Definitely Red." And just like that, her holiday season got a whole lot brighter.

Jack, on the other hand, had quite the problem on his hands.

Chapter Three

Five days later

Bess knew something was up at the conclusion of the Monroe family Thanksgiving dinner, when she and all four of her siblings ended up on the covered porch. It spanned the front of the clan's iconic Triple Canyon Ranch house. Late-afternoon sunshine spilled across the lawn on the beautiful fall day, while she and her two brothers and two sisters sat down on the cushioned wooden chairs. The children and spouses remained inside.

More peculiar still, everyone except her seemed to know what this meeting was all about.

"What is this?" Bess joked, pulling her sweater closer. "An intervention?"

More looks exchanged all around.

"Actually," said Erin, the eldest sibling, who had raised the rest of them after their parents passed, "it kind of is."

Bess wrinkled her nose, sure they were joking. Except…they weren't.

"You all know I don't do drugs or smoke and I rarely drink, so—"

"It's about your private life," said Gavin, the cardiothoracic expert and ER doctor.

The youngest, Nick, who ran the family's famous Western wear clothing store, added, "Specifically, your relationship with Jack McCabe."

Bess stared at them, feeling as if she had somehow ended up in the middle of a very bad reality TV show. "You really disapprove of my friendship with one of the most honorable men around?"

Her twin and fellow nurse, Bridgett, said, "If it were just that, of course we wouldn't object."

"But…" Erin took up the mantle once again. "…it seems like more than that."

Bess only wished. "In what way?" she asked tightly, finding it hard not to be offended.

"In the sense that you are using each other to keep from moving on from your past relationships," Erin went on, "and getting involved with anyone else."

Bess stiffened her spine and glared at her sibs. "Jack isn't interested in getting married again. Everyone knows that. He was already married to the love of his life." And lightning did not strike twice. Jack had said that a lot, too.

"But you *are* interested in finding your Mr. Right and getting hitched," Gavin reminded her. "We only had to read your two Christmas letters to realize that."

Bess cringed. Was there anyone in Laramie who didn't know about that?

"It was a joke," she fibbed, feeling humiliated all over

again. She tried to get the conversation back on track. "Maybe not a very good one, but—"

Nick, who had recently married and had a baby with his true love, said, "It's not just a relationship that you're yearning for. We all know you want a family, too, Bess." Clearing his throat, he continued, "And we all want that for you."

"Which is why," Bridgett announced with a satisfied grin, "we've come up with a plan to not only get you through the holidays, but to help make all your dreams come true, as well."

Shortly after 9:00 p.m. on Thanksgiving Day, Jack parked at the curb in front of Bess's home. To his relief, her car was in the driveway and the lights were on. Realizing this was the first time he had dropped by like this, without checking to make sure it was okay first, he paused. Wondering if he should have called.

Before he could change his mind, the porch light came on, the front door opened and Bess stepped out.

He'd thought, like himself, she might still be in her holiday dinner clothes. Instead, she was wearing a pair of jeans with holes in the knees and a paint-splattered T-shirt that ended just above the low-slung waistband. Her mane of thick wavy brown hair was swept up on the back of her head, and she held a paint roller in her hand.

A quizzical, concerned look adorned her face.

"Everything okay?" she said as she walked down the steps of the porch to her century-old, newly reno-vated shotgun home.

He got out of his SUV and met her halfway. "Yeah. Sorry. I didn't mean to alarm you." As he gazed into her dark green eyes, he had to push aside the sudden desire to kiss her. "I just wanted to talk to you, maybe ask you a favor."

Her shoulders stiffened.

Aware he had upset her, yet not sure why since they did routine favors for each other all the time, he continued, "Is this a bad time?"

She shook off whatever it was. "No." She raked her teeth across her lower lip. "It's fine. Come on in." She whirled on her heel and led the way inside.

The living room and dining area were at the front of the house, the kitchen, walk-in pantry and laundry room were in the middle, and the bathroom and master bedroom behind that. A detached car garage, accessible only from an alley, sat on the other end of her small rectangular backyard, which was enclosed with a new six-foot-high wooden privacy fence.

He and the girls had seen the place when she'd bought it, but he hadn't been back in the nine months since. To say it was transformed was putting it mildly. "Wow," he said, looking around. "New Sheetrock."

Still holding the roller, she propped a fist on her hip. "I had no choice when the chimney collapsed on itself."

"Right. You mentioned that in your glass-half-empty Christmas letter. You didn't tell me about it when it happened."

Her cheeks registered a pretty pink flush. "Home renovation isn't really your thing, though, is it?"

He tracked the strands of silky hair escaping the confines of her messy bun, falling over the nape of her neck and across the upper swell of her breasts. He returned his glance to her face. "No, but…it must have been upsetting."

Carefully, she bent and set the roller back in the paint tray. She strode to the kitchen, stripped off the glove she'd worn on the hand with the roller and dropped it into the trash. She reached up to undo the bun, and her hair fell to her shoulders in loose, dark waves. "Bad enough I had to deal with it," she said, combing the strands into place with her fingers. "I didn't want to bring anybody else down."

Jack ignored the growing pressure at the front of his jeans. "I would have liked to be there for you."

She looked at him for a long, thoughtful moment. "What did you say you wanted to ask me?" She strode past him in a wake of lavender perfume.

Jack figured he'd better concentrate on something else if he didn't want to end up putting the moves on her. "Why are there three colors of paint on the wall in here?"

"I'm trying to decide which neutral shade is the most salable."

He did a double take. "You're planning to sell this place?" After all the work she had put into it over the entire last year? Where would she go? Hopefully, not away from Laramie.

Bess lifted her slender shoulder in an artless shrug. "Eventually. Probably, yeah." A distant look came into her eyes. "When I get married. I mean, it's too small for the kind of family I'd like to have, although Gavin and Violet have made a similar floorplan with a small footprint work by adding a second story to accommodate their two children."

"So you are seeing someone?"

She stared at him, affronted. "Why is the idea of that so shocking?"

Damn, she was irritable tonight. "It's not," he rushed to reassure her. He just didn't want to imagine her with anyone else, for reasons he chose not to examine closely.

"Then...?"

Jack ignored the twinge of something tightening his gut. "I just thought we knew a lot about each other."

She grimaced at his assessment and shook her head. "Well, obviously we don't if any of this surprises you." She huffed out a breath. "Now, for the third time, why did you stop by? You mentioned needing a favor...?"

Guilt rippled through him. Was he taking advantage here? He stepped back. "Maybe now isn't the time to ask."

"After all this buildup, you'd better!" As if realizing how that sounded, she held up a hand. "I'm sorry for being so crabby." She sighed, abruptly looking utterly defeated. "It was just a day."

The urge to take her in his arms and comfort her grew stronger. "Something happen with your family during dinner?"

Bess went to the fridge and got out two bottles of lime-flavored sparkling water. She handed him one. "An intervention. They're all concerned about me and want me to start dating again. And to that end, Bridgett has even fixed me up with Tim Briscoe."

Jack pretended an ease he could not begin to feel. "The new pediatrician at the hospital?" Even as he asked, he knew this was none of his business.

She took a long drink. "Apparently he's had his eye on me."

No surprise there. Bess was beautiful. Talented. Kind. Gentle. Loving. Of course Briscoe wanted to go out with her. Any man in his right mind would.

She paced back and forth, looking on edge. "Better yet, he wants to settle down and start a family as much as I do. And," she added wearily, "he's willing to let himself be fixed up, too, if that will get him what he wants."

He slanted her an assessing look. "What about you?"

She pursed her lips together. "Well, my sibs all seem to think that if I'm ever going to get what I want out of life, I have to get back in the dating pool sooner rather than later. So I said if he asks, I'll go out with him." She paused and studied him, frowning. "What? You don't approve?" She gave him a faintly baiting look. "You think I should just wait for a miracle to happen?"

He thought she should wait until the time, and the man, were right.

"Come on, Jack. You may as well tell me what you think. I'll figure it out anyway."

She probably would—she knew him that well. He shrugged. "Okay, if you want me to be honest, I don't think you should waste your time. Or his. I can already tell the two of you won't click."

Her mouth dropped open in surprise.

He felt the same. What the hell had gotten into him, weighing in on Bess's love life?

She put down her drink and glared up at him. "Well, I don't know what happened to you, either, today, Jack, but I can tell you this. I *really* don't need or want another person telling me just how hard up I am in the romance department!"

Chiding himself for the unwarranted jealousy, Jack searched for some inner nobility that would give Bess what she needed in a friend while satisfying his craving to forge a deeper connection with her. "I didn't say that," he said.

"Really?" She stepped back, all cordial Texas grace. "Because it seems like you're implying that no one would be really interested in me. Never mind find me attractive enough to marry and have children with."

He tried to ignore the erratic intake of her breath and the definition of her breasts beneath the cotton shirt. "Is that what you think?"

She kept her eyes on his. "Yes, it's what I think!" She jammed her finger against the center of his chest, picking up steam with every second. "Furthermore…" Her lower lip formed a delectable pout. "…just because you don't find me the least bit desirable, Jack McCabe, does not mean no one else will."

She really thought he hadn't ever noticed how incredibly sexy and beautiful she was? "Of course I find you desirable," he said. Not that he had ever made a move on her.

She snorted and rolled her eyes. "Yeah, Doc, right."

What had gotten into her? Why was he suddenly the enemy, when all he had ever done was treat her with the kindness, courtesy and respect she deserved? Finding himself beginning to get a little worked up, he lowered his face to her. "You want me to prove it to you?"

Because suddenly he was ready to do just that. And not just to make a point. He studied the skeptical look in her eyes and guessed with even more disappointment, "You don't think I can. Do you?"

She whirled away from him, putting enough distance between them so they were no longer invading each other's personal space. Then she propped her hands on her hips, the action lifting the fabric of her T-shirt.

He did his best to keep his eyes on her face. She obviously had no idea the way her current posture was showcasing the luscious curves of her breasts and the strip of silky abdomen above the waistband of her jeans. That did not mean he was unaware. He could feel himself getting hard. Not good. Not good at all, when they were supposed to be casual friends and nothing more.

Oblivious to his growing reaction to her, she tossed her head, almost as if she were daring him to make a pass at her. Silky hair spilled over her shoulders. "You want me to be honest with you?"

Realizing she wasn't the only one taking unprecedented risks here, he gritted his teeth and did his best to think of everything that was cold. Ice. Snow. Showers when the water heater was on the fritz. Someone bumping into you and spilling a frozen drink all over your lap. "Yes."

Her expression exuded hurt. "Then no," she told him, "I don't think you desire me." She threw up both arms. "And since the last thing that I want right now, Doc, after being pressured into accepting a fixed-up date, is a pity kiss—"

That was it. The last straw. Doing what he had wanted to do from the first moment he had laid eyes on her this evening, he wrapped his arms around her and brought her close enough to feel the wild beating of her heart.

"Damn it, Bess. Don't you get it?" he growled, finally losing all patience. "*Pity* is the last thing I'm feeling." Bending down, his lips hovering right above hers, he admitted softly, "Regret maybe, for waiting this long…"

And he wasn't waiting any longer. He fused his lips to hers, knowing she was everything he could ever want in a woman, and in that instant, he felt their desire for each other confirmed in an undeniably electric way. Though he hadn't meant to do anything other than prove his point, as he heard her first gasp of surprise that swiftly turned into a soft moan of surrender, he knew this kiss…their friendship…was going somewhere. Somewhere good.

Bess had known it was a mistake to throw down the gauntlet with Jack, just as it had been a mistake to let him come in when she was already so overwrought. She should be concentrating on what she needed and had always wanted—a husband and family of her own—instead of succumbing to the pent-up lust she'd been feeling for quite some time.

But she couldn't help it. There was just something so dangerously exciting about Jack's kiss. She reveled in the hard demand of his mouth on hers, the masterful way he held her. She had never been kissed like this, with such fierce possessiveness. Had never felt such need or want welling up inside her. He was so sexy. So masculine. So deliberate and determined. And she knew if she let him continue kissing her, she would have to admit that she had always had a thing for him.

And if she did that, they'd likely end up making love. Which would be fine, more than fine actually, if he could ever really care about her, the way she knew she had the potential to care about him. Unfortunately, there was only room in Jack's heart for one woman: his late wife.

With effort, she broke off the kiss and pushed him away.

He stepped back.

She was breathing hard, tingling all over and perversely longing for more. *So much more.* And that could not happen.

Forcing herself to be realistic, she said, "That was a mistake."

A complex array of emotions crossed his handsome face. "Bess   "

Her heart in turmoil, she stalked to the door and opened it wide. "You really have to go. Now, Jack."

He gave her a long, measuring look. Then, with a curt nod, he did as she asked.

Chapter Four

The last person Bess expected to see on her doorstep the following day was Jack with a tray of pastries and two coffees in hand. Wishing she had done more than wash her face and brush her teeth and put on her painting clothes, which this morning were an old denim work shirt and the same ripped jeans she'd had on the day before, she went to greet him.

He, too, was dressed in old clothes. Worn jeans, running shoes with a rip in them, and funnily enough, an old denim work shirt, too.

Jack spoke first. "I thought you'd be out Black Friday shopping."

And yet here he was, with a scrumptious-looking breakfast for two. With as much equanimity as she could muster, Bess reminded him, "Those sales started weeks ago."

For a long, telling moment, he remained motionless,

seeming not even to breathe. He definitely wasn't backing down. He nodded. "True."

Not ready to forgive him for tempting her with what they both knew they could never have—and walk away unscathed, anyway—she remained in the doorway, arms folded. "So what's up?" she asked, not sure whether she wanted to smack him or haul him close and kiss him all over again. She may not come to her senses and stop this time.

He leaned in a little more. "I want to apologize."

Like groveling would help, now that she knew just how good he tasted and how big and strong and right he felt pressed up against her.

She paused an uncomfortable length of time. "For?"

Looking like he, too, wanted to say the hell with talking, take her in his arms and kiss her passionately, he drawled, "You're not going to make this easy on me, are you, darlin'?"

"Nope."

He looked her up and down, as if considering his options as carefully as she had been. "You going to invite me in?"

Her pulse racing, she lifted her shoulder in a careless shrug. "Depends on that apology."

He exhaled. "Okay." Something dangerous glittering in his eyes, he said, "I shouldn't have kissed you."

Bess noted with mixed feelings that he wasn't saying he would never do it again.

Seeming to realize he was getting nowhere fast, Jack said, "Not like that, anyway."

Like you wanted to take my breath away? Guess what, Doc—you did.

"You mean…passionately?"

He winced. "To prove a point."

Grimacing, Bess said, "Can't argue with you there." She noticed that her neighbors to her left, a kindly elderly couple who had taken it upon themselves to watch over her, had suddenly come out to take the cornucopia off their front door and hang up a wreath. The simple chore was taking an inordinate amount of time. Wondering how much they'd seen or could potentially overhear, and deciding she and Jack didn't need to put on the kind of fireworks that would compel the happily married couple to intervene on her behalf, or worse, play matchmaker, she moved aside to usher Jack in and shut the door behind them.

He walked over to the dining table, set down his offering and took off his coat. Then turned back to her, his expression as genuine and honest as his low tone. "I'm not sorry I did."

Of course he wasn't, Bess thought, even more aggrieved, because it wasn't his heart that would end up broken.

"Well, there we do differ, Doc," Bess said, lifting her chin. "Because it can't ever happen again."

Jack knew he'd screwed up, giving in to his temper. Acting on desire in the heat of the moment. But he hadn't expected her to hold a grudge that would continue to keep them apart, for more than a few hours, anyway. "Why do you say that?" he asked.

Bess got out plates, silverware and napkins. She brought them over to the table. "Because it could ruin our friendship."

Her pronouncement struck a chord. He thought about a life without Bess in it. How lonely it would feel. He sat down opposite her. "I wouldn't want that."

She took the top off her coffee cup and sipped her vanilla latte. "Then we're in agreement?" She studied him over the rim of the cup. "We're not going to kiss again."

To his disappointment, Jack saw there was no convincing her otherwise. For now, anyway.

He removed the lid on his own coffee. "Yes." The best way to get their relationship back on track was to spend time together, platonically, and build on that. "And to make it up to you," he said, "I'm prepared to help you paint."

She cut into her cherry cheese Danish. "You don't have to do that."

He bit into a pumpkin scone, swallowed, then inclined his head. "Actually, I think I probably do."

Slowly, recognition dawned. "Don't tell me. You've got another favor to ask of me, the one you intended to hit me with last night?"

He sat back in his chair, wondering what it would be like to have breakfast with her like this every morning. "You got it."

Bess surveyed him as they ate.

She'd swept her hair loosely into a clip on the back of her head, tendrils escaped around her cheeks, down the nape of her neck. The subtle makeup she usually wore was absent. Her freshly scrubbed face looked younger and more vulnerable, her lips bare and soft, and he longed to explore the silky texture.

Oblivious to the effect she had on him, she batted her lashes at him mischievously and asked, "Does this have anything to do with Christmas?"

He mimed a blow to his heart. "You are psychic," he teased.

"When it comes to you, maybe I'm just experienced," she bantered.

Still sitting kitty-corner from her at the table, he

watched her take another bite of pastry. Actually, she wasn't nearly as experienced with him as she thought. Otherwise, she'd have known he'd been lusting after her for two years now. He'd just been too wary of taking advantage of her vulnerability to act on it. Especially since he knew he no longer had the romantic idealism in him that would allow him to believe in happily-ever-after the way she did—with all her heart and soul.

Still hungry, he tried a chocolate croissant.

Bess helped herself to an apple, oatmeal and walnut breakfast cookie. "So, is Santa coming to your house this year instead of your parents' ranch?"

"He is."

Warmth flowed through him at the look of open admiration in her beautiful green eyes. The feeling intensified as she leaned forward in a drift of lavender perfume to nudge the back of his hand with her elbow. "Good for you."

He hoped so. He still wasn't entirely sure he could pull off Christmas on his own. At least not with the panache Gayle had. He didn't want to let down his kids.

"What about the puppy?" she persisted, her teeth raking her lower lip.

Wishing he actually could kiss her again without battle erupting, Jack admitted, "Santa's apparently bringing one, too, that is just like the puppies they met at Winfield Retrievers. Only definitely not one of those."

"Except it will be," Bess concluded.

"Yes." He carefully met her gaze. "Which is where we come to the problem. Those puppies are going to be ready to be picked up on December 19. And Betty is adamant they go to their new residence at precisely eight weeks."

Bess set her empty cup down. "Which is going to be an entire week too early for your purposes."

"Yes."

Another thoughtful pause. "Betty knows your situation?"

"She is willing to make a slight exception by letting me pick up our pup and temporarily house her elsewhere. Provided, of course, I keep our new puppy close by and personally bond with her every day until she comes home on Christmas morning."

Bess's delicate brow furrowed. Rising gracefully, she began to clear the table. "How are you planning to do that?"

Here came the tough part. Jack left the remaining pastries in the bakery box and carried them to the kitchen. He stood next to her at the kitchen sink. "I was hoping you might agree to keep both puppies here for a week. I know you've already planned to take two weeks of vacation to help acclimate yours. And I only have the week between Christmas and New Year's off."

It was hard to tell what she was thinking. He added hastily, "I'd help out with both pups, of course. We just wouldn't be able to let the girls know they were here."

Slowly, Bess got the same blissed-out look on her face she'd had when picking out her puppy. "Sure."

This had been almost too easy. He studied her, wondering all the while if he was taking advantage, which was the last thing he wanted. "You really don't mind?"

Her smile spread. She bent over to put their plates in the dishwasher, the hem of her shirt riding up her shapely thighs as she did so. "No, not at all. Maybe the two pups will keep each other entertained, while they get used to doing without their mother and the other littermates."

He lounged against the counter, watching her, unable to do anything else to help. "Thank you." He heaved a big sigh of relief.

"What are friends for?" she retorted. "I am curious, however." She tipped her face up to his, in much the same way she had before he had kissed her last night. "What are you going to do about Chloe's present?"

Jack's gut tightened. "The only thing I can. Convince her to want something else other than a real live baby brother."

Bess's heart went out to Jack. The death of his wife just three days after the birth of his youngest child had sent him reeling.

Knowing, however, that they had to get a move on if she wanted to get her living room finished, she handed him a paint roller. Then she knelt to pour more light gray paint into the pan, enough for the both of them to use. "I don't suppose there's any way to explain to a three-year-old that you can't just order up a son the way you do a new toy." She supposed he had already tried, to no avail.

"Or even a healthy, easy pregnancy," Jack replied gruffly.

Bess froze. This was the first time he had ever talked about this with her. "Gayle's last two pregnancies were exceptionally difficult," she recalled, walking off to get a trim brush.

He began spreading paint on the wall. "If it had been up to me, she never would have gotten pregnant a third time."

This she hadn't known. Edging the walls, she asked carefully, "What do you mean?"

Jack moved the roller up and down with smooth,

rhythmic strokes. "When Gayle was diagnosed with placenta previa—"

Which carried the risk of severe bleeding during pregnancy and delivery, Bess knew.

"—during her second pregnancy and put on bedrest, I wanted to go ahead and get a vasectomy, so we would never have to worry about her getting pregnant again."

"She didn't agree?"

He shrugged, the fabric of his faded shirt molding to his broad shoulders and muscular chest. "She wanted me to keep our options open, in case something went wrong with either the birth or the pregnancy. So we'd have another chance at having a second child."

That sounded like Gayle, who had been a stellar physician in her own right. Complications alone would not have scared her. "So you passed on the procedure," Bess guessed. She noted he hadn't yet shaved. The stubble on his jaw gave him a rugged, sexy look.

"Then." He moved back to the tray, to replenish the paint on his roller.

"And that changed...?"

His mouth took on a hard, uncompromising line. "When she accidentally got pregnant with Chloe a few months after giving birth to Nicole, I just went ahead and did it."

That, too, sounded like Jack, not wanting to take any more chances with the health of the woman who had been the love of his life. She moved close enough to see the heat in his eyes. "How did Gayle feel about that?"

Suddenly, Jack appeared as if he had the weight of the world on his shoulders. "She was furious. And when she found out we were having another daughter, instead of the son she was convinced I had to have, she was even more upset with me."

"Aside from the gender issue…" A nonissue, as far as Bess was concerned. A healthy baby of either sex was the goal. "…you can't really blame her for being angry about the vasectomy, Jack. That was a decision the two of you should have made together."

"Except she never would have made it," he pointed out.

True. Still… Bess watched him wipe the edge of the roller to prevent it from splattering paint. "Did she ever forgive you?"

Jack's gaze turned brooding. "Not really. Although her anger lessened when she was diagnosed with placenta abruption with her third pregnancy."

An even more difficult complication to weather, Beth knew, because it put the life of both baby and mother at tremendous risk.

"She had to go on bedrest a second time, when we already had a six-month-old and a two-and-a-half-year-old to care for." He stopped, shook his head.

"It must have been hard for you."

He rubbed at the back of his neck with his free hand. "The bane of being in the medical profession. You know all too well everything that can go wrong."

"Except it didn't seem to affect Gayle," Bess recalled.

"I don't know if it was the fact she was an ob-gyn and thought she could manage her own situation as effectively as she cared for any of her patients, or if it was just denial."

"Because she didn't want to really consider the risks," she guessed.

Jack painted another section of wall. "She never doubted that Chloe would be born on time and healthy."

"And she was." Bess recalled the giddy relief of those

first few happy days. Followed by almost unspeakable tragedy.

"Right." Jack swallowed. He set the roller in the tray. "It wasn't Chloe's life, it was Gayle's life that was put in jeopardy with post-birth hemorrhaging. And then when she survived that…" His voice trailed off. He was unable to go on. Eyes filling, he turned away.

Her heart going out to him, Bess set down her brush. She approached him gently, sympathizing, "It had to have been awful for you, arriving at the hospital to take her and the baby home, only to find out she'd suffered a pulmonary embolism just minutes before."

Face ashen, he nodded.

"It wasn't your fault, Jack," she said fiercely.

Before she could hug him, he moved away. Shoulders tense, he retorted, "Yeah, Bess, it was. Because if I'd just had the vasectomy when I first wanted to, Gayle never would have become pregnant a third time, and she never would have died."

Jack's heartrending confession resonated with her. She knew he had been haunted by his wife's death. She just hadn't known the specific reasons why.

Now she did. And while it was a relief, the new information was also a burden. It left her with so many more questions. Just like the one he'd asked her, the week before, after reading her two Christmas letters.

She approached him once again, putting a comforting hand on his forearm and guiding him around to face her.

"Is this why you don't date?" *Because you blame yourself?* "Because you don't want to let anyone else down?" Or was it deeper than that? She stepped even closer. Pressed, even more softly, "Or is it because once you've had the best, you don't ever want to settle for second?"

Which was, quite frankly, what she or any other woman would be in his life.

Good question, Jack thought, recoating the roller and painting the last section of wall with long, smooth strokes. And one whose answer had definitely changed since he had found himself butting into Bess's personal business. Given in to impulse. Kissed her.

Of course, as fate would have it, she'd come to her senses and called a halt to their steamy embrace. That told him something, too. They needed to be direct with each other. And cautious.

After all, they could both still get hurt here.

Aware she was still staring at him, patiently awaiting his answer, he cleared his throat. "I haven't wanted to date because, at first, I was so grief stricken I couldn't imagine myself with anyone but Gayle."

Bess nodded, accepting that.

"Then, as time passed and the mourning subsided and I was finally able to accept everything, I was too busy." Or at least he had told himself that every time he noticed just how beautiful and sexy Bess was.

"And now?"

Still lusting after you, darlin'. Sensing she would not want to hear that, though, he said merely, "I'm taking it one step at a time."

He definitely wanted a second kiss with Bess. Maybe even a third, if it helped make their holiday season a little merrier. Beyond that, was it fair to pursue her, given what she ultimately wanted? A husband and a baby of her own?

He could give Bess a lot. Could he give her that? Even half of that?

Right now…did he have to? Maybe it would be enough to start paying her back for some of her many kindnesses the last three years.

"And speaking of taking it one day at a time…" He set his roller down in the tray and wiped his hands on the rag. "Now that this is done, do you have plans for the rest of the day?"

Looking as ready to put the tragedy of the past behind them as he was, she lifted her chin. "Really, Doc?" she countered sassily. "You need *another* favor?"

"Actually," he said, crossing to her side to take her hands in his, "the girls and I'd like to do one for you. Maybe help you get a Christmas tree? Bring it back and set it up?"

Chapter Five

"But you have to get a Christmas tree!" Nicole protested, when Bess met up with them later at the Kiwanis lot set up in a big field on the outskirts of town.

Lindsay looked at Bess, crestfallen. "You'll be sad without one."

Bess pivoted, expecting Jack to help her out. Instead, he shrugged, as if to say the girls sort of had a point. "Are you sure having a puppy precludes one?"

"Yes," she said firmly, breathing in the lovely scent of all the evergreen trees.

Although that wasn't the only reason she didn't want one. She feared having a tree this year could make her melancholy, and she was currently taking steps...a lot of steps...after her two-letters screwup to avoid just that.

With a sincere smile, she volunteered, "But I can still help you all pick out yours." His three girls could be a lot to handle in the midst of a busy tree lot the day after Thanksgiving. "So what did you have in mind? Big or little? Green or flocked in white?"

Chloe and Nicole slipped their hands in hers, while Lindsay, who at six felt she was too big to have to hold someone's hand in a public place, moved close enough to Jack he would not worry. "It's got to be big enough so it's taller than Daddy," Lindsay declared.

Which meant over six feet four inches tall, Bess noted.

"Why is that, sweetheart?" Perplexed, Jack looked down at his oldest.

"Because, Daddy," Lindsay explained, "trees have to be bigger than the people. That way, you have to stand on your tippy toes or get a chair to stand on to put the star on top."

"But," Nicole countered importantly, "not so big there is no room for the presents and the puppy Santa is going to bring me."

Chloe beamed up at Bess. "It has to be just right!"

Jack's gaze met Bess's over the tops of his little girls' heads. When he looked at her like that, like the kind, loving dad he was, she couldn't help but smile back.

"Sounds like we have a plan, then," he mused.

Half an hour and many rejected pines later, they had an actual tree for Jack's place. As they headed home, the bevy of questions continued.

"Can we put the lights on tonight, Daddy?"

"Sure. As long as it doesn't get too late."

"Can Bess help?"

She lifted a hand, setting the limits on that inquiry herself. "I'll help you get it inside and in the stand. Maybe put the lights on."

"Then we can have pizza!" Nicole shouted happily. "'Cause it's Friday!"

"Can Bess stay for pizza, Daddy?" Chloe asked.

"Sure, if she wants to," Jack said.

Did she? The times she did stay, she always felt like part of their family unit. Which was dangerous emotionally, because she wasn't. But if she left or passed on the opportunity to be with them, she often felt bereft. So she was really on the fence, trying to figure out what would be best on that particular night.

Luckily, she didn't have to give an answer right away, because Jack was turning onto Spring Street.

As soon as they got the stand and tree inside, the questions started again. "When do you get your puppy?" Lindsay asked.

Bess knelt to hold the stand still while Jack fitted the trunk in the bottom of the metal holder. "Three weeks."

Jack motioned for the two of them to change places, so she stood and grabbed on to the trunk while he knelt at her feet. "What are you going to name her?" Chloe asked.

Bess leaned her body to the left while Jack reached around, beside and behind her, tightening the screws. She looked down at his thick dark hair, still tousled from the winter wind. "I haven't decided yet. But I'm thinking about calling her Grace."

"We're going to name the puppy Santa brings us after Mommy. And her real name was Abigayle, not Gayle, and Daddy always said Mommy was pretty as a princess. So we're going to call her Princess Abigayle."

This was apparently news to Jack. Although after a moment's tension, he seemed to take it in stride.

"So you should call your dog Princess Grace," Nicole concluded.

"Ah." Bess and Jack exchanged glances, once again of the very same mind.

"Not a good idea." Jack went to get water for the tree.

Lindsay scowled. "Why not?"

"Oh, um." A whole host of reasons. Starting with the fact the real-life Princess Grace suffered a particularly tragic ending. "Because…" Bess made it up as she went. "…we would want our dogs to have pretty different names, so they wouldn't get confused." She caught Jack's nod of approval as he returned, then turned back to the girls. "But we could call her Lady Grace." A registered purebred, her new pup was going to need several names anyway.

"I like that." Jack smiled.

"Princess Abigayle and Lady Grace," Lindsay said, smiling, too. "Can they have playdates?"

Bess took a leap of faith. "Probably."

"You know, we don't know for sure that Santa is going to be able to bring you a puppy," Jack said. After adding water, he draped the base with a skirt. Bess knelt to help him straighten it. "But," he continued, "I think there might still be time. We could still get one from Mrs. Winfield."

Thereby negating Bess's need to secretly babysit their puppy until Christmas morning. Which would certainly cut back on temptation, she thought.

"No, Santa's going to bring us a puppy!" Chloe said stubbornly.

"And come down the chimney and put it under our tree!" Lindsay chimed in. "Or he will when we send him our letters. Daddy, when are we going to send him our letters?"

Jack frowned. "I think you need to work on them some more. Maybe ask for a few more things, so that if he doesn't have something…"

Like a real live baby brother, Bess thought.

"…he can bring you something else and you will still be happy with it."

"Like a mommy?" Chloe asked, innocent as ever.

Bess felt Jack's pain. Doing her best to keep her expression gentle, she steered his daughter in another direction. "Or some new dress-up clothing. Like the princess gowns they have in *Frozen*." One of the girls' favorite movies, they had watched it together countless times.

Chloe perked up. "They have those?"

"I think so." Bess sat down and whipped out her phone. "Let's see if I can find a picture." She typed in the request, then scrolled through the images that popped up.

"Those are pretty," Chloe said, cuddling close on the sofa.

Bess wrapped her arm around the child, realizing all over again how much she wanted a family of her own. "I think so, too."

Chloe sucked on her thumb. "Can I ask Santa for one?"

"I'm sure you can," Bess soothed, trying hard not to see how relieved Jack looked.

"And a real live baby brother and a mommy," Chloe added.

"So much for asking them to add to their wish lists," Jack said later, when he and Bess were carrying the empty ornament storage containers back out to the garage.

She shrugged, looking lovely despite her dishevelment. But then, three hours of marathon tree decorating with three little ones could do that to you.

Seeming to realize her hair was slipping out of its

clip yet again, she released it. "At least the things they each picked out online are gettable."

He nodded, still feeling a little overwhelmed. Not Bess, though; this all seemed right up her alley. He moved the stepladder over to the high wooden shelf that ran along the perimeter of the garage.

"And you did explain to them that none of them will get absolutely everything on their lists," Bess told him. "So that will help."

She handed him a plastic storage box and he moved a few steps up to put it on the shelf. Jack exhaled in frustration. "It'd be a tad easier if Lindsay and Nicole weren't going to see their most heartfelt wishes—of getting a new puppy and having Santa visit our house this year—come true. And Chloe weren't still hooked on the idea of getting a new mommy and a real live baby brother."

Bess sent him a sympathetic glance. "Because Chloe still won't be getting what she ultimately wants from Saint Nick. Whereas her two older sisters will."

"Right. And none of the items that Chloe picked out online...not the princess costume or the easel or the new baking set for her play kitchen...are going to come close to what her sisters are receiving from Santa. At least in emotional terms."

"I know." Bess sighed, briefly looking as stymied as he felt. "It is a thorny situation. But there's still time to come up with a solution."

"I just wish I intuitively knew a little more about what little girls liked in terms of toys and stuff, so I wouldn't always feel so out-of-my-depth in situations like this. And could instinctively come up with a present that would dazzle Chloe so much it would make up for the fact that—" he was forced to clear his throat

"—she and her sisters don't have a mother. And won't ever have a baby brother." Even though…in some perfect world…he could see himself wanting a complete family again, too.

Sadness came and went in Bess's eyes, the way it always did when the topic of his late wife came up. Motioning for him to stay put, she went on tiptoe to hand him another. "Can't your sister help you?"

He relieved Bess of her burden with a smile of thanks. Noticing how the long tunic and leggings she'd changed into post-painting molded to her slender torso, he said, "Lulu and Sam have their hands full with their triplets now."

"Your mom?"

As he reached down to get yet another plastic storage container, he couldn't help but note how the scoop neckline of her top gaped slightly as she worked, revealing the curves of her breasts. "She thinks if I'm planning to stay single that I need to either research and learn about gifts for little girls on my own or ask some of my female friends for help."

Glad they were done, he came back down the ladder.

Bess stepped out of his way. "Do you think that's a way of getting you back out there, dating again?"

Jack closed the ladder. "Maybe. Everyone I know expects me to marry again." He paused, looking down at her. "Except you."

Looking beautiful and kissable and sympathetic as all get-out, Bess met his eyes. "Falling in love isn't the kind of thing you can fake. Or simply conjure up by wish. If it were, well—" she shrugged "—let's just say I would have been hitched a long time ago."

He returned the ladder to its place. "But you still want to be."

Suddenly, her mood became as cautious as his. "In theory. If the man and the situation were right. Of course I would."

He was aware all over again just how little he knew about what was in her heart. "And until then?"

"I really don't want to settle, Jack. I've done that before."

Doing his best to respect the parameters she had set, which meant not giving her the physical hug she seemed to need, he guessed, "With the guy you were engaged to marry."

"Until he realized he still loved his prior girlfriend, anyway. Not that it was really a surprise, in retrospect."

He lifted his brow.

Ignoring his gentle prodding, she lifted her chin and speared him with a testy gaze. "I had two other serious boyfriends before then. One in high school and one in college. Both were all in when we were dating. Then they left me, because they still weren't over their previous girlfriends and didn't honestly know if they would ever be. So—" she blew out a frustrated breath "—no more rebound romances for me. If I want a family, and I do, I'm going to have to build one another way. Starting with my new puppy."

Who was destined to bring her much happiness. That, he knew. "Are you really going to call her Lady Grace?" he asked, before the barriers around her heart went all the way up again.

Bess relaxed. The corners of her lips tipped up into an inviting smile. "I think so. Kind of has a ring to it." She slid her hands into the pockets of her tunic. "What about you and Princess Abigayle?"

He fell in step beside her. They closed the door on

the detached garage and headed for the house. "It also has a ring to it."

"It won't remind you too much of Gayle?"

Jack shook his head. He would always miss his wife, but the overwhelming sadness was gone. "No one ever called her by her full name. So, no." And if it helped his girls feel closer to their mother, he was all for it. As they moved up the steps of his Victorian, he looked over at Bess. "Nice save with Chloe, by the way."

"You're welcome."

Their gazes intersected. The moment drew out. And all Jack could think about was kissing her again. "So are you joining us for pizza tonight?"

"Thanks," Bess said, "but I need to get home. Get that wreath I bought today decorated and on the front door."

They continued on into the house. The girls were sitting at their craft table in the family room, coloring more pictures to include with their letters to Santa.

For not the first time, Jack found himself hating to see Bess go. "Got plans for tomorrow?"

Looking both happy and relieved, Bess admitted, "As a matter of fact, Doc, I do."

"I wish Bess could have stayed for dinner," Lindsay lamented as Jack set out the pizza.

With Mrs. D. off with her own family for Thanksgiving weekend, it was just him and the three girls. And though it was normally cozy and sweet, tonight it definitely felt like something—or someone—was missing. To the girls, too?

"Bess explained why she couldn't stay." With a reassuring smile, Jack doled out slices to Lindsay and Nicole and cut Chloe's pizza into pieces. "She's going out

of town with her two sisters for the rest of the weekend."
He helped himself to a couple of pieces.

Lindsay picked melted cheese off her pizza and popped
it into her mouth. "What are they going to do?"

"I don't know." Jack savored the mix of ingredients
on his pie as he took a healthy bite. "She didn't say." And
her deliberate mysteriousness was not like her. But then,
maybe there was still a lot he didn't know about Bess.
And should.

To his consternation, he didn't hear a word from Bess
all weekend. He didn't see her at the hospital Monday
morning, either, so he went to the staff cafeteria over
lunch, hoping to run into her there.

No such luck.

He was just about to get up from the table when Tim
Briscoe approached him. Unlike the surgical staff, who
all wore scrubs, the young pediatrician was dressed in
a shirt and tie, perfectly creased slacks and suede loaf-
ers. His thick auburn hair was as neatly arranged as
his clothes.

"Got a minute, Jack?" he asked. Barely thirty, he
looked as green as most physicians fresh out of resi-
dency.

"Sure." Always willing to help a colleague, Jack gestured for him to have a seat.

With a huff of relief, Tim put down his tray and settled opposite him. "I finally got Bess Monroe to agree
to go out with me."

Jack felt a strange sensation in his gut.

"I know the two of you are friends," Tim continued,
earnest as ever. "And I need some advice."

Reminding himself that at the end of the day all he
wanted was for Bess to be happy, Jack forced himself

to be as chivalrous as his mother had raised him to be. "How can I help?"

"Well, I was going to take her to The Wagon Wheel restaurant for dinner, but then I ran into her this morning and realized if I want to have a chance with her, I'm really going to have to up my game."

"What do you mean?" Jack asked, his shoulders tensing. What was wrong with one of the nicest restaurants in Laramie?

"You haven't seen her today?"

"Ah...no."

"Well..." Tim stopped and broke into a wide grin. "There she is."

Jack turned toward the entrance. Bess was there, all right. Dressed in the trim black uniform the rehab nurses wore. Looking gorgeous as could be.

And not at all like he remembered her.

She'd had her hair cut to chin length. Gold and caramel highlights shimmered in the sexy, tousled waves. Her makeup was different, too. Still subtle, but sexier somehow.

Really, really sexy, he noted on a wistful sigh.

"Hey, man, watch my tray for me, will you?" Tim said and rushed off to greet her.

Bess smiled as Tim approached. He accompanied her through the line, talking and flirting openly all the while. Getting her to smile. Laugh. Shake her head in amusement. He even tried—unsuccessfully, it appeared—to pay for her lunch. She had it packed up to go.

Jealousy coursing through him, Jack watched as the two stood talking for a moment longer. Then Bess gave Jack a small wave hello before she headed back out the door, clear plastic salad container and drink in hand.

Tim came back to the table. "She has to get caught up on her paperwork, so she's going to eat at her desk."

Jack wanted to think it was a likely story, that Bess just didn't want to spend time with the eager young doctor and Jack simultaneously. But he knew it was probably true. Bess often worked straight through lunch.

Tim sat down. "So," he concluded, "you can see now why I suddenly think I need to up my game."

Chapter Six

Eight hours later, the girls were asleep, and Mrs. D. had settled down in front of the television. Too restless to prepare for the seminar he was giving at the Veterans Healthcare Summit in Dallas later in the week, Jack headed out to the detached garage.

He had just opened up the overhead door when he saw Bess out on a jog. It wasn't unusual for her to run past his house; the residential part of historic Laramie had a labyrinth of quiet, tree-lined streets perfect for that purpose.

With a nod of acknowledgment, he headed toward her. Watched as she slowed her pace and came to a halt just in front of him. Clad in pink-and-white leggings, a zip-front hoodie and sneakers, her new haircut held back from her face by a pink headband, she looked as fit and sexy as ever.

Ignoring the urge to take her in his arms, Jack said,

"A little late to be working out, isn't it?" Usually, she got her miles in right after work.

Bess admitted this was so with an inclination of her head. "I, um, wanted to talk to you."

That was a good sign, wasn't it?

Maybe not, given the sudden rueful twist of her lips. Still working to catch her breath, she put her hands on her hips. "So I figured I'd wait until after the girls were in bed."

"Which they are."

"Okay, then." She lifted her chin. "Are you the one who told Tim he needed to take me to The Laramie Inn for our first date?" she asked.

So he was playing matchmaker now? He put his hands on his waist. "No."

"Then what were the two of you talking about at lunch?"

Unsure if he was betraying a confidence or not, Jack said hesitantly, "Briscoe asked me some questions about local eateries."

The swell of Bess's breasts rose and fell as she continued to slow the meter of her breath. "And you said…?"

With effort, he returned his gaze to her face. "The Laramie Inn is probably the nicest place around within a thirty-mile radius that wouldn't involve driving all the way to San Antonio or Dallas."

Her soft lips took on a downward slant. "Well, now he's taking me there," she reported unhappily.

Jack struggled to contain his envy. "And that's a problem because…?"

"Going somewhere that fancy puts a lot of pressure on the date."

Easy solution there. "So don't go." He dragged the

shipping boxes, full of unassembled yard ornaments, to the center of the garage.

She followed him inside. "I have to."

Methodically, he used a pair of scissors to cut through the mailing tape on the top of every box. "Why? If you're already having second thoughts?"

She walked around after him, keeping her voice low. "Because Erin and Bridgett are right. I'm never going to get what I want if I don't start putting myself out there again."

He went to the spare fridge, got out a bottle of water and tossed it to her. Putting his own unwarranted jealousy aside, he advised, "Then go and have a good time."

She uncapped the top and drank thirstily. Her eyes glittering with an emotion he could not identify, she studied him over the rim of the bottle. "You mean that?"

No, Jack thought. *Actually, I don't want you to go. And I really don't want you to have a great time. And I really, really don't want to know what that says about me and my own selfishness where you are concerned.*

Forcing himself to sound much calmer than he actually felt, he said, "You deserve to be loved. We all do. And if Tim Briscoe is the guy who can provide that…"

She watched him take the pieces out of the boxes and set them on the garage floor. Her irritation apparently dissipating, she said, "Sorry. I'm just a bundle of nerves today."

As was he. He walked close enough to inhale the lavender of her perfume. "You didn't enjoy your weekend with your sisters?"

Bess lit up like the decorations already out on his street. Moving back and forth, probably to keep her muscles from tightening up, she said, "Actually, we had a great time. We went shopping and bought new dresses for the holiday. And then they gifted me a full day at the spa. Which, thanks to all the money I've been spending on my house and new puppy, I couldn't begin to have afforded on my own."

"Ah." He took the opportunity to leisurely peruse her new, sophisticated appearance. "That's responsible for the hair?"

She wrinkled her nose, slipping back into trusted friend mode. Fluffing the ends comically, she asked, "Well, Doc, what do you think? Do you like it?"

Oh, yeah, he liked it. He really liked it. Not trusting himself to speak, however, he merely nodded.

She peered at him. "You don't think it's too...?"

Sexy? Hell no. "Definitely not," he said, sidestepping her obvious worry. "In fact," he added gruffly, "it's perfect."

If Bess didn't know better, she would think from the way he had just been looking at her that Jack was thinking about kissing her again. Knowing that would be a mistake, she gestured at the yard ornaments he was removing from the boxes. "What's all this?"

Looking handsome as ever in a navy plaid flannel shirt and jeans, Jack exhaled. "The girls are worried Santa won't be able to find our house, since he has 'never been here before,' at least that they recall. And they also want to decorate our yard on the outside this year, so I was hoping to take care of both things in one fell swoop."

Bess knelt and looked at the photo on the outside of the boxes. "'Charlie Brown and the Gang and The Musical Christmas Tree,'" she read aloud, smiling. "Wow, the girls are going to love this."

"It's their favorite holiday program."

She grinned. "I'm aware." She had sat on Jack's sofa and watched it with them numerous times. "Lindsay especially identifies with Charlie Brown's melancholy."

"I know." Jack shook his head, looking slightly melancholy himself. "She says Charlie is just like her daddy—he starts out sad at Christmastime and then gets 'all happy in the end.'"

True, unfortunately. Bess surveyed her old friend, head to toe. "You seem to be doing better this year."

Jack perked up. "Think so?"

She nodded, easily slipping back into her sidekick role. "Just the fact you're willing to do this…" She gestured at the two-foot-high figurines and the much larger Charlie Brown tree he was trying to wrestle out of the box. She moved in to give him a hand.

They brought out the comically spindly tree with the sparse drooping limbs, along with the ornaments. Jack furrowed his brow, as if suddenly not sure this was going to be so great after all.

Bess knew it was. "Want me to help you set this up outside?"

"Your run…"

Unwilling to admit just how much she wanted to spend time with him, at least for a little while longer, she shrugged. "Exercise is exercise."

His gray-blue eyes sparkled with self-deprecating humor. "Sure. I'd love your help."

The next half hour was spent finding the perfect place in the yard for the display and then anchoring the tree with green metal stakes pushed deep into the ground. When that was done, they arranged Lucy, Linus, Snoopy, Charlie Brown, Peppermint Patty and Sally around the tree, and then hooked it all up to an outdoor surge protector. Jack held up the end of the cord. "Ready?"

"More than." Bess grinned.

He plugged it in.

The whole display lit up.

"It's gorgeous," she breathed.

He came to stand beside her. Then took her hand and drew her closer. On the back of the Charlie Brown character, there was a switch. He turned it on. The sounds of "Hark! The Herald Angels Sing" filled the air.

"Wow."

And just that quickly, the feel of Christmas was upon them. They stood for a moment, drinking it all in. Ignoring the residual heat from his powerful body, not to mention her spiraling desire, she said, "The girls are really, really going to love this."

Jack gazed down at her. Something real and intense shimmered between them. As the moment drew out, he gave her the look that said what he really, really wanted was to haul her close and kiss her all over again.

He cleared his throat and he stepped back. Once again, he respected the parameters they had set. "So." He picked up a few tools. Then they headed back to retrieve the water bottles they had set down a while back. "When are you going on that date with Tim Briscoe?"

Talk about breaking the mood! "Wednesday evening."

He quirked a brow in surprise. "Why not the weekend?"

Feeling restless and in need of a long, hard, adrenaline-draining run again, Bess capped her bottle. "Because I won't be here. I'm going to the Veterans Healthcare Summit in Dallas on Thursday."

"You didn't want to wait until the following weekend?"

Didn't great minds think alike. Now that Bess had agreed—more like, been pressured—into going out with someone else again, all she wanted to do was delay it. Indefinitely. But the more practical side of her knew that wouldn't help. So now she just wanted to get it over with. Which was not a great thing to be thinking in advance of the date, she thought guiltily.

Still, she knew her sisters were right. She'd never be able to move on from her previous failed engagement, and this crush she had on Jack, unless she pushed herself.

She cleared the frog from her throat and explained, "I won't be back from the conference until late Saturday afternoon at the earliest. Tim's got weekend call. So Wednesday was the best we could do unless we wanted to put it off another ten days, and neither of us did."

Jack nodded. An indecipherable emotion came and went in his eyes. "Well. I hope you have a good time."

Bess did, too.

She didn't know how long she could keep lusting after a guy who had vowed never ever to marry again.

At ten thirty Wednesday evening, after a perfectly pleasant but painfully long date, Bess sat quietly as Tim Briscoe parked his BMW in front of her home and cut the engine. He turned to her with a mixture of hope and regret. "Tell me the truth," he said softly, reaching over to take her hand in his. "Would it have made any difference if I had taken you somewhere…anywhere else…this evening?"

She knew what he was asking and chose to evade. "The Laramie Inn is lovely."

Tim's profile was handsome in the glow of the street-light. "No question, our meal was perfect." He paused and let go of her fingers. Down the block, holiday lights twinkled merrily. "It was the chemistry that was lacking."

Bess drew a breath. As much as she wanted to assuage his ego, it wouldn't do either of them any good for her to lie. She pressed her lips together regretfully. "I wanted us to click."

"So did I. But…" Tim released his seat belt and moved to get out. "…sometimes the necessary sparks aren't there."

Bess waited for him to open her door for her, the way he had all evening. "We could be friends," she volunteered as they moved up the walk.

He staggered comically, thumped his heart with his fist and groaned in dismay.

Bess couldn't help but laugh.

"Anything but that!" he lamented.

This time, she caught *his* hand as they moved up the steps to her porch. He was funny and charming, and—on paper, anyway—everything she could want in a man. Except one thing. He wasn't Jack.

She tried again. "I'm serious, Tim. I'd like to get to know you better. Introduce you around." When he hesitated, she persisted, "Unlike you, I grew up here. I still know all the single gals. One of whom might very well be the perfect woman for you."

He tilted his head, considering. "You'd do that for me?"

"Matchmake? Heck yes!" As the idea hit and her guilt faded, Bess leaned in close to whisper, "And this is how we're going to do it…"

Jack's plan was to bump into Bess as she was coming into work Thursday morning, and do what he could to learn how her date with Tim Briscoe had gone the evening before.

Did he have competition? Had they set up another date? If they hadn't…as he hoped…that meant the way for him was clear. He could pursue her without stepping on another guy's turf.

And he *did* want to pursue her, he had decided.

It was the only way they would ever know if they were meant to be more than friends.

Unfortunately, he was called in at shortly after two o'clock that morning for an emergency surgery. Another followed. When he went to the staff cafeteria for lunch, Bess was there, all right, seated intimately close to Tim Briscoe, their heads bent over her phone.

Disgruntled, he realized their date had probably gone better than even Tim had expected. Had he lost his chance with Bess? There was no way to know.

Except that the two sure looked thick as thieves now.

Neither Bess nor Tim looked up once. Just as well. With the jealousy roiling around inside him, Jack would have had a hard time behaving.

Clenching his jaw, he grabbed a two-liter bottle of water and a protein bar and headed back up to his office to eat in solitude.

Luckily, work consumed him for the rest of the afternoon.

By the time he had finished the two surgeries previously scheduled for that day, it was five o'clock, and he had to head home to pack up and get ready for the next day's seminar in Dallas.

His mother was in the kitchen sitting at the table, doing something crafty and Christmassy with his three girls that seemed to involve a lot of glitter, construction paper, scissors and glue.

"Get done early today?" he asked, already knowing the answer. Since Gayle had passed, his tax attorney mother managed to sneak away from the office around four a couple of times a week, to spend a little time with her granddaughters before heading out to the ranch where she and his dad lived.

Rachel smiled. "Unlike you." She paused in concern. "I hear you were up all night."

Mrs. Deaver busied herself at the stove, leaving the hefty lifting—of dissuading him from his previous plans—for his mom.

"Please tell me you're not planning to drive to Dallas tonight after the exhausting day you've had," Rachel said.

She needn't have worried. She wasn't the only one who didn't want him to fall asleep at the wheel.

"Way ahead of you, Mom. I already called Garrett Lockhart—" former army doc and now physician-CEO "—at the West Texas Warriors Association, to see if I could hitch a ride with the group of attendees they have going."

Of which, coincidentally, Bess was a member. As was he. And many others of the medical and former military professionals in town. All of whom worked to help current, wounded, and retiring military veterans and their families.

"Oh." Rachel sagged with relief.

Jack glanced at his watch. "Unfortunately, the WTWA van will be here any minute, so…"

He raced up the stairs to grab his duffel bag and garment bag, which he'd packed earlier, then raced back down to the study to collect the data he needed for his presentation. He was just zipping up his laptop case when the doorbell rang.

"Your ride is here," his mother called smugly from the foyer.

Only, as it turned out, it wasn't the entire contingent from WTWA.

It was just Bess.

Chapter Seven

"Everything okay?" he greeted her as she came up the walk. Adorned in black jeans, fancy Western boots, a white silky blouse and a fitted evergreen suede jacket, she looked pretty as a picture.

Flashing a casual smile, she joined him on the porch. "We had two too many for the van, so I volunteered to drive and take you, since the two of us were both running late anyway."

"That's thoughtful of you." More than thoughtful, actually. It was an amazing stroke of good luck. "Thanks," he said, ushering her inside.

Bess cocked her head, taking his gratitude in stride. "No problem," she returned affably.

As always, his daughters were delighted to see their favorite family friend. All spoke at once.

"Hi, Bess."

"Can I have a hug?"

"Why are you here?"

She seemed to blossom with all the attention. "Hi, everyone. Of course you can have a hug." She knelt and engulfed all three girls in her arms, smiled hello at his mom and Mrs. D. "I'm here to drive your daddy to Dallas for the conference."

"Daddy!" His three girls surrounded him before he could get a word in edgewise. "You can't go yet! Not before we mail our letters to Santa Claus! You said we could go to the post office and do it with you!"

He broke eye contact with Bess and turned back to his girls, reminding them, "We aren't done with those yet."

"Yes, we are! I said I wanted Santa to come down our chimney!" Lindsay declared.

"And I wanted Santa to bring me a new puppy!" Nicole chimed in. "Just like the one Bess is getting, only *not that one!*"

It was all Jack could do not to cringe, although Bess's expression remained remarkably nonchalant.

"And I want a mommy and a baby brother!" Chloe claimed.

He tensed.

Luckily for them all, his mom stepped in. "I was just explaining to the girls that Santa can't bring real people."

"But he brings real puppies!" Chloe argued.

"Maybe," Bess said, "it would be a good idea…just in case Santa doesn't have what you all want at his toy shop at the North Pole this year…to ask Santa Claus if he would bring you all surprises instead."

The girls paused.

Jack sent Bess a grateful glance only she could see. "Brilliant," he mouthed.

Chloe clapped her hands. "We love surprises!"

"Yes, we do!" Nicole agreed.

"As long as he brings them here to our house," Lindsay said.

Eager to have this resolved, he said, "Sounds like we have a plan, then."

The girls retrieved their letters. The adults helped them add "a surprise" to their lists, which were folded into the envelopes addressed to the North Pole, along with the pictures the girls had drawn earlier.

"Daddy," Nicole declared, "we need stamps."

Jack went into his office and returned with a book of them. He doled them out. The girls carefully pasted them on.

"Can we please go to the post office?" Lindsay asked.

"Now?" Nicole echoed.

"I want to put them in the box!" Chloe added.

Jack looked at Bess. This was turning into quite the ordeal. Not that his self-appointed driver seemed to mind. She was as chipper as always when she was around his girls. "We've got time since it's just the two of us," she said.

"Five!" Lindsay corrected, counting. "There are five of us who are going to go."

Jack exhaled. There were times when being a dad seemed almost more than he could handle on his own. Thank heaven for Bess's cheerful, steady presence.

He smiled at his girls. "Right again."

Bess couldn't help but note as they all climbed inside Jack's SUV that he looked exhausted. "Want me to drive?" she asked.

"If you don't mind. Yeah."

They made it to the post office in downtown Laramie just before the 6:00 p.m. closing. The girls carried their letters inside and, standing on tiptoe, pushed them over the counter.

The fiftysomething postal clerk smiled when he saw the address. "I suppose you want these mailed off right away?"

"Yes, please!" the girls said in unison.

"Will they get there in time?" Lindsay asked.

"Plenty of time," the clerk assured her.

The girls were sober as they left. "Maybe you should write Santa a letter, Daddy," Lindsay said as they piled back into his car.

Wondering what this was about, Bess backed out of the space.

"Maybe then," Chloe said, "if Santa brings you what you really want, you'll be happy."

Nicole piped up from the back seat. "You, too, Bess!"

She sighed. Out of the mouths of babes.

But his kids were right. Jack had been looking a little stressed lately. Not as stressed as she had been when she'd written the two Christmas letters. But like he was missing something in his life, too.

"You know," Jack's mom said as they went back in to retrieve his belongings, "your father and I will have the kids starting tomorrow evening. So if you or Bess were to decide you needed a little more time in the city…for holiday activities…it'll be perfectly fine."

Jack accepted the offer with an inscrutable nod. They said goodbyes to everyone, then walked out to Bess's Volvo sedan. She opened up the trunk, and he stowed his duffel and garment bag in the trunk.

"Sorry about that," Jack said.

Unable to help herself, Bess quipped, "The delay in leaving or the obvious matchmaking?"

"Both," he deadpanned.

Key in hand, she slid behind the wheel, wishing her own mom were still alive to give her such grief. "She wants you to be happy."

A mixture of resentment and resignation warred on his handsome face. "Doesn't everybody." Then he pressed his fingers to his eyes and grimaced in self-recrimination. "Now who's sounding Grinchy?"

Bess knew what it was like to work what amounted to a double shift and go twenty-four hours with little sleep. "Hey." She reached over to pat his arm. "You've got a right to be a little grouchy."

Not that he seemed all the worse for wear for it, though. He had a day's beard rimming his ruggedly chiseled jaw, his dark brown hair was rumpled, but his cobalt blue eyes were as alert as ever despite the shadows of fatigue beneath them.

"In fact," she continued, unable to help but admire how his big body seemed to take up the entire passenger side, "I don't mind if you want to sleep while I drive."

As generous to a fault as usual, he said, "I'd rather hear about your day."

"Not much to tell. We were busy all day in the rehabilitation clinic. There's a lot of excitement about the upcoming holidays. Which is nice."

As was driving, with him by her side.

Jack smiled, as if he relished the chance to talk with her. "You seem happy, too."

"I guess I am."

His gaze roved her face. "Is it because of your date last night?"

Cool segue. Bess accelerated as she merged onto the highway. "In a roundabout way."

Jack turned to her, waiting.

Aware he still looked better than anyone had a right to look after such a long day, Bess smiled and said, "I'm going to help Tim find someone. Or at least I'm going to try. We were working on who he might want to be introduced to today at lunch. Luckily, the lady in question was amenable, so I've already set something up."

He flexed his shoulders beneath his cashmere sweater. "So you're not seeing him again?"

"Only as a friend."

Was it her imagination or did that news please him? From the loaded silence, something was clearly on his mind. "What?" she asked, slanting him a quick glance.

"I'm your friend," he pointed out drolly.

"And…?"

He said nothing.

Her heart rate accelerating, Bess tried again. "What are you asking?"

Jack folded his arms. Stared straight ahead. "If you kissed him."

Whoa. "Not that it's any of your business, Doc, but no," she rasped. "We did not!"

Jack kept his poker face.

"We had a perfectly nice date, and I really enjoyed spending time with Tim," she finished in exasperation, wishing she'd been able to say more.

"Then?"

A palpable silence fell. "Neither of us was feeling it."

He nodded, complacent.

Her irritation rose. "You don't have to look so happy about it."

"I'm not."

Ha! It was her turn to wait for him to continue.

Eventually, he said, "I just never saw the two of you as a couple."

Nor had Bess, if the truth were told. Deciding she wanted answers, too, she pointed out, "Yet you were helpful to Tim when he came to you for advice."

Another shrug of those broad masculine shoulders. "I try to be supportive."

Supportive. Was that what she wanted?

He turned as much as his seat belt allowed. The fabric of his slacks molded to his rock-hard thighs. "Would you have rather I acted like a jerk about it?"

Would she? Did she want him to be jealous of the idea of her with another man? And what if he was? What exactly would that prove? Bess kept her eyes on the road. "Of course not."

He caught the low note of pique. "I'm not trying to irritate you."

Deciding the passenger compartment had become way too hot and close, their conversation suddenly far too intimate, she turned the car's thermostat down another four degrees and said, "I know that, too." She continued driving. Five miles passed, then ten.

In the distance, horses grazed in the moonlight. The next pasture up, it was cattle.

"So what is your plan for your love life?" he asked. His low tone said she could tell him anything and he would understand.

Her mind made up on this issue, she gripped the steering wheel tightly with both hands and admitted candidly, "I don't really have one. Except to know I'm not going to date anyone just for the sake of dating them again. If the sparks aren't there, I'm not going to waste my time. Or his."

Jack felt a lot of things about Bess's pronouncement. Relief, that he didn't have any competition to worry about, at least in the short term. At least he hoped. Given how attractive she was, her single status was certainly not guaranteed.

And guilt, because as much as he lusted after her and yearned to make her his, he knew he could not give her what she wanted most. The promise of everlasting love and marriage and a baby of her own.

All of that had been wrung out of him when he lost his wife. He no longer believed that everything would always work out the way he hoped. Instead he'd learned the hard way that life was a crapshoot. And Bess deserved more than a relationship with someone who no longer had the soul-deep hope and faith to make all her dreams come true.

"Jack?" Bess's voice jarred him from his thoughts. "I want to fuel up before we hit the city. There are several fast-food places up ahead. Do you want to get something to eat now, too?"

Getting out of the close quarters of the car suddenly seemed like a very good idea. He turned to her with a smile. "I do."

Fifteen minutes later, they sat down opposite each other at one of the Formica-topped tables next to the window. Popular Christmas music played in the background. A lit tree decorated the ordering area.

"By the way," he said as they unwrapped their sandwiches, "I meant to thank you for broaching the idea of asking Santa Claus for a surprise gift. When did you come up with that?"

She beamed. "Right then, actually."

He gave her half his fries; she gave him half her onion rings. "Gayle used to be able to do that with the girls. I never have really had the hang of it."

She cut her grilled chicken sandwich in half with a

plastic knife. "Don't sell yourself short. You're a very good father to them."

It helped to hear her say it. "Thanks," he said quietly, although today was one of those days when he felt like anything but a great dad. The fatigue of the long day beginning to hit him, he took a bite of his cheeseburger.

"It's all going to work out."

He grimaced. "Once I come up with the ideas for those surprises they asked Santa for..." Something spectacular enough to make them forget they did not have a mother. Right now, he was drawing a blank.

Bess nodded, almost as if she knew something. Which, given her expertise in dealing with his three daughters, she probably did.

"Any thoughts?" he asked.

Her smile sparkled almost as much as her eyes. "A few," she teased.

Loving the way she looked when she got excited about something, he leaned back in his chair and studied her over the rim of his cup. "I'm listening."

"Well..." She drew an enervating breath that lifted the swell of her breasts. "To make it fair, you could have Santa leave a note for them, saying he was gifting all three of them the visit to their house and the new puppy. Then, for the surprise gifts, do something really special and equitable for each one of them."

"Like...?" Gazing into her emerald green eyes, Jack pushed aside the sudden desire to take her hand in his and hold tight.

"Chloe mentioned one of her friends has a really nice dollhouse that is apparently three stories high and around four feet tall."

Jack took another long, thirsty drink of his iced tea and considered the effects of sibling rivalry. "If Santa got Chloe that, I think the other two would each want one, too. As long as they were all different, that is."

Bess's grin morphed into a satisfied smile. She tucked an errant strand of silky hair behind her ear. "I don't think that would be a problem."

Jack imagined it would not.

In an effort to get comfortable in a chair that was several inches too short, he shifted his legs beneath the tabletop, bumping her knees with his. Tingling from the accidental brush of their legs, he drew back. "But what would I give them from me, then, that would match up with what Santa's done?" Make them feel loved and appreciated on both counts?

"How about some really spectacular new baby dolls? Picked out to go with their new dollhouses?"

He finished his burger and dragged a french fry through the ketchup. Deep down, he knew they had all been leaning on Bess too much, especially him, but it was hard not to when she was so much fun to be around. "Sounds good."

Finished with their meal, they stood and carried their trays to the bin, then walked back to the drink machines to refill their cups. "Where would we get all of this, though?" He gestured for her to go first.

Bess stepped to his right, bumping him a little in the process. "I'm not sure about the dollhouses." She added more ice and soda to her cup. "I'll call some of my friends with little girls and ask if they can recommend any particular vendor. As for the dolls, that will be easy. There's a big doll store for little girls in the Galleria mall in Dallas."

Trying not to notice how right it felt to be here with her like this, without other family to act as chaperones, Jack looked down at her. "If we pull this off," he predicted huskily, "the girls will be thrilled."

"I think so, too." Together, they walked outside to her car. Standing in the cold air, waiting for her to unlock the door to let them in, Jack had the strong urge to pull her in his arms and kiss her.

For both their sakes, he did not. He stared down at her, wishing attraction and affection were as uncomplicated and easy for adults as they were teens. Because if they were...he and Bess would have been an item a long time ago. "Thanks for all the help."

She opened the driver door and climbed in. "You're welcome."

No sooner had they gotten back on the highway again than Jack got a call. He answered. Then he said, "Hang on. Let me ask." He muted the call, then said, "It's my speaking partner for the conference. She wants to go over the material we're covering in the seminar tomorrow. Would it be okay with you if we did this now, over the phone?"

Glad not to be the sole focus of the sexy surgeon's attention, Bess replied, "Have at it. All I'm going to be doing is driving."

"Thanks." Jack got back on his call. "We're good to go..."

He talked surgical techniques and recovery times until they got close to the Dallas city limits. Then he navigated for her until they got to the hotel. A valet took her car, the bellhop their bags, and they headed inside.

The lobby of the hotel was gorgeous, with high ceilings, marble floors and sumptuous furniture. A beautifully lit twenty-foot-tall Christmas tree stood in the center of the atrium, and soft carols played over the intercom.

What was not quite so Christmassy? The very long line at the check-in desk.

When they finally reached the counter, the clerk scanned his computer and frowned. "We don't seem to have any regular rooms left. In fact," he continued, typing rapidly, "we're sold out for the next two nights."

Bess and Jack exchanged astonished looks.

"How is that possible?" Jack asked.

"We're here for the Veterans Healthcare Summit. We both have reservations," Bess said. Hers was printed out; Jack's was on his phone.

The clerk, an officious-looking man in his late thirties, straightened. "Not everyone we were expecting to check out this morning left."

"And how exactly is that our problem?" Jack asked, beginning to look a little irate.

The clerk got the message. He typed some more. Finally, he said, "If you are willing to share, I can give you a one-bedroom suite with a sitting room that has a pullout sofa. Or we can start calling other hotels in the area and see if they have any availability, but there's no guarantee that will work out, either."

Noting Jack looked like he was going to collapse with fatigue, Bess jumped in. They were adults, as well as old friends. They could make this work. "We'll take the suite here."

Jack lifted a brow, but he didn't seem to be objecting. Just surprised.

She reassured him with a touch to his arm. "What's important is that we're both here and can attend the conference."

"Agreed," Jack said, an inscrutable look on his face.

They finished checking in at the desk, then went up to the room. It was smaller than they had expected. The bedroom was barely able to fit a king-size bed and a wall-mounted TV. The sitting room had a nice view of the city lights, a love seat, with the aforementioned pullout bed inside, and a desk and chair. The bathroom located in between was on the small side, too, but nice, with a spa-like shower.

Quickly, she volunteered, "I'll take the pullout." Even without being extended, Bess could see there was no way a man as big as Jack would fit comfortably on the twin-size bed within the love seat.

"No. I will."

Bess figured they could argue about it later. In the meantime, she wanted to find out about the dollhouses, so they could get started looking for those. "Do you mind if I call some of my friends who have little girls, before it gets any later?"

"I appreciate the help."

She got out her computer tablet and phone and sat down at the desk in the sitting room. He moved into the bedroom, presumably to give her privacy.

She notified everyone she could think of. It wasn't long before the calls, emails and texts started coming in. Twenty minutes and several conversations later, she had a good idea where to start looking and, more important, what features they might want to search for.

Bess hung up and went to tell Jack. He was sitting propped up against the headboard on the bed, fast asleep.

Chapter Eight

Jack woke with a start. A cursory inspection of his surroundings revealed he was lying propped up against the headboard on a king-size bed, in what looked like a hotel room. It was dark outside. And he was fully dressed except for his shoes. A blanket had been drawn across his lap.

The door was partway open. Lights were still on in the next room, and he could hear the murmur of a woman questioning someone. Bess?

As the melodic sound of her voice flowed over him, it all came flooding back. He scrubbed a hand over his face and got up. Moved soundlessly to the door until he was able to see her talking on her cell, with her back to him. He turned away, eased his toiletries bag from his duffel and went into the bathroom.

By the time he came out again, she was off the phone and sitting at the desk in the living area of the suite, her head bent as she made notes on the paper next to her tablet.

He stood there for a moment, awed by her beauty, just drinking her in. Damn, but she was captivating, no matter what time of day or night, no matter what the situation. She'd changed into a knee-length cranberry-red-and-white-striped nightshirt and oversize white sleep cardigan. Her chin-length hair was twisted up into a loose sexy knot on the back of her head, lips bare, her complexion freshly scrubbed and glowing.

"Hey."

She looked up in surprise. "You're awake."

And aroused. He came closer. Stopping just short of her, he inhaled a whiff of her sweet lavender scent. "Was I not supposed to be?"

"Not really." She looked him over, lingering just a millisecond too long on the apex of his jeans, before returning to his face. "I expected you to sleep until morning."

Willing his body to calm down, he slid his hands in his pockets, pushing the fabric out. "Nah." He glanced at her tablet. The screen was filled with dollhouses, normally something guaranteed to make his eyes glaze over. Able to see that it had the opposite effect on her, he asked casually, "Any luck?"

Bess leaned back in her chair. Clasped her fingers together and stretched her arms out over her head. "Oh, yes," she reported happily, still stretching the kinks out of her lithe body. "In fact—" she dropped her hands and stood so he could see her tablet "—I was amazed at how many choices there are now."

Already overwhelmed, Jack groaned.

She edged closer. "What?"

He peered down at her. "When it comes to shopping," he informed her ruefully, scraping a hand beneath the stubble on his jaw, "too many choices can be as bad as too few."

"Not in this case." She beckoned him with a come-hither look. "Want to see?"

He watched as she leaned over and began flipping through a dozen bookmarked pages. The sight of the nightshirt inching up her thigh was as enticing and feminine as the rest of her.

Oblivious to the lusty direction of his thoughts, she murmured, "I think any of these would do for Chloe."

Jack forced himself to get back on task. "Mmm-hmm."

She scrolled through another dozen images. "These would be good for Lindsay." More. "These for Nicole."

Aware he had to get his mind off what a desirable woman she was if they were to platonically share a hotel suite, he went to the mini fridge. After perusing the contents with more than necessary care, he removed a sparkling water and a pack of chocolate-covered almonds. Politely looking over his shoulder, he asked her, "Want something?"

She picked up her tablet and held it in front of her like a shield, thereby blocking his view of the swell of her breasts. "Any more of those?"

"Yeah." He handed her both. Bedtime snack in hand, he settled on the sofa. "Tell me you have some favorites already. Please."

She laughed at the comical expression on his face, then sat down next to him so he could see the screen. The action caused her nightshirt to ride up past her knees. Sliding one hand beneath the tablet on her lap, she discreetly tugged it down. She teased him, "I guess having you look at dollhouses is kind of like having me look at toy construction trucks."

"You have something against big machines?"

"You know what they say." Her elegant brows knit together. "If you've seen one, you've seen them all."

He chuckled, as he knew she'd meant him to, his awareness of her increasing by leaps and bounds with every second. Reminding himself they were both adults, and practical ones at that, he pushed desire aside. "So, what do you think would be best?" he asked.

She got right back on task. "For Chloe, I think it's between these two." She showed him two dollhouses, one a Craftsman style.

Jack decided, "I think she'd like the Victorian, because it looks the most like our house."

"Agreed. Lindsay is getting sophisticated, so she might like the two-story city loft, with the retail shops beneath."

"Very cool."

"And Nicole's very pet-oriented these days, so maybe the Southern traditional that comes with cats and dogs and pet doors?"

"Also nice." He paused. "What about the furniture and the people?"

"All will have the furniture and accessories pictured. And all three of these will fit the size dolls that come from the specialty store we're going to visit on Saturday."

Jack nodded. He turned toward her, his knee accidentally bumping her cotton-covered thigh. "Last question. Can we get them in time?"

Bess sat all the way back against the sofa cushions, then shifted her upper body slightly to face him. "That's who I was talking to on the phone," she said, pleased.

"All the ones you want are currently in stock. With expedited shipping, you can have them next week. But of course they recommend you order as soon as possible because the most popular tend to sell out."

He pulled his wallet from his back pocket and got out his credit card. "Is it okay with you if we use your tablet to place the order?"

"Happy to help. And by the way, if you want to have the dollhouses shipped to my place, I can store them in my garage until Christmas."

Short minutes later, the order was placed, the confirmation going to his email. She shut her tablet. Jack smiled his gratitude, wishing there were some way to repay her for all that she had done for him. "I'm going to owe you a steak dinner for all of this."

She rose. "Or another bag of chocolate-covered almonds." Winking, she started to move away.

He laughed and stood. Catching her hand before she could ease away, he held her in place and looked at her in all seriousness. "I mean it, Bess," he said softly. "I owe you for all your help."

Bess knew Jack wanted to repay her. She wanted to find a way to express her gratitude, too, for the way he had confronted her over the two Christmas letters, then gently but firmly forced her to look at her attitude and change it. He'd encouraged her to make this her happiest, instead of her loneliest, yuletide yet.

"Just tell me what you want, need…" he continued, gazing down at her earnestly.

Desire fluttered inside her, more potent than ever. "You're serious," she whispered.

He nodded. "Yes."

Then there was only one thing that would make the

month of December complete, Bess knew. Only one thing that would ease their mutual loneliness for just one night. She rose on tiptoe, wrapped her arms around his broad shoulders and said, "This."

He drew her all the way into his arms and tunneled his hands through her hair.

Defiantly, she held the challenge in his eyes.

"Sure?" he rasped.

"Very." Reassuring herself this did not *have* to change anything—not for long, anyway—she shrugged out of her sleep cardigan, let it fall to the floor. She let out a shuddering breath as she lifted her face to his.

The gentlemanly, protective side of him seemed to be warring with their mututal desire for sex. He stroked his thumb across her lips. "Bess…" He regarded her ardently, a sense of purpose in his eyes. "If we get started…"

"I know we're not going to stop, but here's the thing, Doc," she said as she pressed the softness of her body against the hardness of his and felt the heat and strength of his arousal. "I don't want to stop."

Nor, apparently, did he.

Their lips met in an explosion of heat and need, yearning and passion. She put everything she had into the kiss, adjusting her lips to just the right angle. Exploring his mouth, tasting his tongue with her own.

The kiss he gave her in return was hungry and wet and unbearably evocative. Taking command, he kissed her again and again, until she was lost in the touch and taste and feel of him. Lost in the ragged intake of their breaths, the chorus of their low, shuddering moans.

Jack hadn't expected this to happen. Not here, not tonight. But now that it was, now that she was in his arms, kissing and holding him tight, he could not fail to see this through. Maybe they didn't want the same things out of life, he reflected as he eased his hands beneath her nightshirt and found the temptation of her breasts, the enticing slope of her abdomen, the sweet silkiness of her inner thighs. But they did have a connection between them that was deeper and more enduring than anything he had ever imagined.

As she let everything she wanted come through in another soul-searing kiss, he realized what she seemed to know already, that happiness during the holiday season was not so far out of reach after all.

Excitement building inside him, he explored and caressed, and her body shuddered and yielded against his. He let all he wanted come through in another long, heated kiss. As he finished undressing her and drew her down onto the sheets, then stripped down and joined her there, she seemed to want more than just sex, too.

He shifted so she lay over top of him. An ache spread outward from his groin. He could feel her nipples beading against his bare chest. She rubbed up against him as they kissed, the softness of her thighs brushing over his.

She wanted to hurry.

He wanted to take his time.

So he did, shifting again so she was stretched out on her back.

"Beautiful," he whispered, rubbing his thumbs across the dusky crowns of her breasts. He cupped their weight in his palms, then kissed his way down, from the V of her collarbone, across the soft swells, to the valley in between. Her skin heated as he suckled gently.

"Jack," she gasped.

"I know." He chuckled, tenderly caressing her stomach, moving lower. "I'm getting there."

He adored her with silken brushes of his fingertips, soothing strokes of his palms, light strokes of his lips and tongue. She surrendered until she lost herself completely in the pleasure. When her quaking stopped, he moved upward once again, the merging of their bodies as electric as the joining of their lips. She wrapped herself around him, taking him deeper.

And then there was no more holding back. The desire they felt dissolved into wild, carnal pleasure. They were lost. Free-falling into an ecstasy that connected them as never before.

Afterward, they clung together. "Regrets?" Jack asked.

Nipples taut, her breath still coming erratically, Bess tensed for a long moment and then sat up. She slanted him a brisk smile that definitely spelled trouble. Averting her eyes, she shook her head, as if her desire had disappeared as quickly as it had appeared. "Not as long as we both understand what this was."

Destiny? Not in her view, apparently. He studied her kiss-swollen lips and the deliciously tousled state of the silky waves of hair, and the desire to make love to her all over again hit him hard and fierce.

"Fun?" he parried lightly, giving her the room to pretend she wasn't anywhere near as romantic deep down as he knew her to be.

She reached for her nightshirt and drew it over her head, covering her gorgeous body from view. "Well, that," she admitted mildly, slipping from the bed. She snatched up her panties and sleep sweater, too, holding them in hand. "As well as a way to relieve some sexual tension and alleviate the curiosity about what it might be like to come together this way."

Jack knew the key to making sure this happened again was ensuring they kept this as informal as they both needed it to be. Ignoring the instinctive urge to haul her back into his arms and kiss her senseless once again, he lounged against the pillows. "And now that we've done that?" He sensed it would be a mistake to push her on this.

"Had our gloriously thrilling and wonderful one-off?" She picked up where he left off. Sobering slightly, she looked him in the eye and said, "I think we need to accept that if our friendship is going to continue unabated, we can't let this happen again."

Chapter Nine

If Jack had any ideas about Bess changing her mind, she quickly put them to rest. First, she disappeared into the bathroom, then came out and made up the sofa bed.

It already had sheets on it, but he moved to help her with the blanket and pillows. "I'll sleep out here."

She lifted her chin. "It's more my size than yours. So I'm calling it."

Argue? Or be a gentleman and let her have her way? He let his gaze drift over her one last time. "Okay," he relented. "But if you change your mind…"

The stubborn set of her chin superseded the vulnerable sheen in her green eyes. "I won't." Fingers curling around his shoulder, she aimed him toward the bedroom. "Get some sleep, Doc," she advised dryly. "I sure plan to."

He tried. Despite his fatigue and the surge of post-sex endorphins, sleep would not come. Not for him. Or, judging by Bess's quiet restlessness, for her, either.

Finally, he drifted off around 2:00 a.m.

When his alarm went off at six thirty, she was already up and dressed in a figure-hugging green cashmere sweater, a trim knee-length black skirt, matching tights and flats. The chin-length waves of her gold-and-caramel-streaked hair had been artfully styled, and sophisticated makeup applied.

She offered a cordial smile as she swung a black carryall over her arm. "I've got a breakfast meeting, so the suite's all yours."

"Thanks." Before he could ask her if she was free for lunch, she was gone.

And so it went for the rest of the day.

She appeared on the panel regarding nursing care for veterans at the same time he was prepping to teach the three-hour afternoon session on surgical repair.

At noon, he checked the ballroom where the lunch buffet was being held, but did not see her anywhere. By the time he got back to the suite to get ready for the evening banquet, he had already missed her again. He knew, because the shower was damp and the suite smelled of her soap and perfume.

By the time he had cleaned up and changed, and called home to talk to his parents and check on how all three of his girls were doing in his absence, it was time for the meal to start.

Seating for the Friday evening dinner was assigned. He was at the table for the surgeons who'd had speaking gigs that day. Bess was with the West Texas Warriors Association contingent from Laramie County, where she regularly volunteered, as did he. They were clear on the other side of the room.

He was still dealing with his disappointment over that when fellow surgeon Celine Ross came up from behind and grabbed his arm. "Jack!" she whispered in his ear. "You're over here, dude."

He knew. He just didn't want to be.

Not when Bess was elsewhere.

He dug in his heels, said pleasantly, "I was going to say hello to someone."

Celine shook her head. "You'll have to do that later. They're starting."

So they were, Jack noted as the ballroom lights dimmed.

Bess usually enjoyed the Veterans Healthcare Summit, the highlight of which was usually the speeches given during the banquet on Friday evening.

Not this year.

As compelling as the personal stories, problems and solutions were, she could not pay attention for the life of her.

All she could focus on was the sight of Jack, a distance away, sandwiched between two really gorgeous women, both of whom, it seemed, were vying for his full attention.

As the meal concluded, Lucille Lockhart leaned close. "Are you feeling okay, dear?" asked the philanthropist, whose charitable foundation funded the WTWA.

Bess shook herself out of her funk and forced a smile. "Of course! Why do you ask?"

Lucille peered at her with obvious concern. "You're usually so lively. Tonight you've hardly said a word."

"Sorry." Bess struggled with her mixed feelings of guilt and frustration and tried to get her mood back on track. "I have a lot on my mind."

"Anything I can do?" the lovely sixtysomething widow asked.

No, Bess thought as she said her good-nights and headed off, but there was something *she* could do. If it wasn't too late.

Unfortunately, moving through the ballroom took longer than she'd hoped. By the time she reached Jack, he was exiting the ballroom, the two women on either side of him, linking arms with him.

"…such great music in Deep Elum…we're all going… it'd be the perfect way to celebrate the great seminar we gave today…"

Oblivious to the fact she was behind him, Jack continued with them, down the hallway, past the elevators and into the lobby, toward the exit.

Bess knew she could race to catch up, somehow insinuate herself into the group and possibly into the outing, as well. But somehow it didn't seem worth it.

Besides, after the way she had summarily dismissed him the night before, what if he didn't want to see her? What if, instead, he was looking for more rebound fun? If he were, she knew she only had herself to blame. She could have spent last night locked in his arms, had she only been brave enough to take him up on his invitation. But she hadn't been. Once again she had made the wrong decision in the moment and missed out on an opportunity for happiness.

With a sigh, she ducked away from the crowd and into the nearest elevator. Then she let herself into the suite, where Jack's clothing was in as much disarray as hers. She promptly burst into tears.

Ten minutes later, Jack opened the door to the suite. Bess was sitting on the love seat. She was still wearing the sexy scarlet cocktail dress and heels she'd had on earlier. She had a crumpled tissue in hand. Her cheeks were pink, her pretty face stained with tears.

"What's going on?" he asked in alarm.

"Nothing." She jumped, as if startled, and turned toward him in chagrin. Rising, both hands knit in front of her, she admitted, "I didn't expect you to be back."

He studied the agonized expression on her face. "And yet I am." He closed the distance between them and took her trembling hand in his. "Seriously, darlin', what's got you so upset? Has something happened?"

She sighed tremulously, fighting back a fresh wave of tears, and buried her face in her hands. "No, no."

"Then…?"

Her lower lip quivering, she dropped her hands, pivoted and paced away. She stood staring out at the glittering array of city lights visible through the hotel window. Her expression was troubled. "I'm just having a moment."

He looked around until he found a box of tissues, then brought her a fistful and shoved them into her hand. "The holidays got you down again?"

Jack wasn't sure whether the sound that escaped her was a pent-up sob or a bitter laugh. "Something like that."

Given that it appeared to be some kind of man trouble, and he knew he hadn't done anything to hurt her, he put his arm around her shoulders and asked gruffly, "This doesn't have anything to do with Tim Briscoe, does it?"

Bess drew in another halting breath and turned, her soft body brushing his. "Honestly? I told you that Tim and I were just going to be friends." She shook her head and put up her hands as if to ward him off. "I probably just need to wash my face and go to bed."

He couldn't stand the raw vulnerability in her gaze. He moved to block her path. "Please don't shut me out like that. Gayle used to do it whenever she was upset with me, and it drove me crazy."

Bess paused to blot the moisture from her face. "What makes you think you have anything to do with this?"

Jack shrugged. He might not know what was going on, but he sensed by the way Bess was continuing to react to him that he was somehow in the middle of it. "Instinct," he replied.

She straightened. "Why are you even back here?" she countered unhappily. "Why aren't you out on the town?"

So she was jealous? That was a twist. "Because I hate clubbing." Surveying the new wave of color coming into her face, he asked, "Why aren't you out on the town?"

She stepped nearer. "Because I hate clubbing."

They smiled.

"It makes me feel really rural and small town," Bess continued.

Absolutely nothing wrong with that. Small-town values like hard work, family and community were the very foundation of his life. "So," Jack said, "that's something else we have in common." He worked off his tie, tossed off his jacket. "I promise, I'm a good listener."

"I know. It's just…embarrassing."

Settling in for a long talk, he undid the first couple of buttons of his shirt, rolled up his sleeves. "I've had my share of embarrassing times, too."

"Well, I thought I had managed not to be so all-over-the-place emotionally this year during the holidays. That there weren't going to be as many crazy ups and downs, that I would be on more of an even keel."

He walked over to the minibar. "That's pretty much the holidays, isn't it?"

Bess kicked off her shoes and settled on the love seat. "Not for Bridgett."

"Really?" He pulled out two beers and a couple of packages of peanuts. "'Cause I could have sworn I heard your sister complaining about her swollen ankles and heartburn the other day at the hospital."

"Well, that's just because she's pregnant." Bess curled her legs up underneath her, spreading out the skirt of her dress around her. "It's very unusual for Bridgett to grouse about anything."

"Okay, then what about me?"

Bess scoffed. "You're fine."

"Really?" He handed her a chilled beer, then unscrewed the top of the other one. "Guess you missed me stressing over what to get the girls for Christmas, when what I really should have been doing was exalting over the fact that I have three lovely daughters to buy gifts for."

She conceded this with a small smile.

Jack clinked bottles with her. "My point is, darlin'…" They both paused to sip. "…December is a month of heightened emotions for everyone. You've got to stop being so tough on yourself."

Her normal good humor crept back into her smile. "All right, all right, Doc, I'll try."

He opened up the packet of peanuts and spilled some into her palm. "Now, as to your hit from the green-eyed monster, that was kind of cute."

Bess winced. "It was embarrassing."

"Then we're even." He ate a few peanuts. "Because as you recall, I've had the same reaction to Tim Briscoe."

"Nothing happening there," she reiterated.

"And nothing happening with me and anyone else, either," Jack said in the same stern tone. "So." He let his gaze drift over the delicate features of her face. "Back to my original question, darlin'. What had you crying your heart out tonight?"

For a moment, he thought she wasn't going to answer. Then, her expression full of that steely determination he knew so well, she asked, "You really want to know?"

He caught her wrist and felt her pulse quicken beneath his fingertips. "Yeah, I really do."

She inhaled. "I think I made a mistake telling you that I only wanted to make love with you once."

He kept his eyes locked with hers. "It wasn't true?" Hot damn, he had hoped as much.

"Nope." Her expression turned droll. "Not in the least."

Jack couldn't help but note how pretty she looked, with her fresh, glowing skin, bright eyes and kissably soft lips. "Then why did you say it?"

"Because I thought you might regret our rebound fling and that it could become really awkward, and I wanted to give you an easy out."

They exchanged rueful smiles. He tore his glance from her lips with effort. "The only thing I regret is not being honest with you last night. I didn't want us to be one and done, either."

She stood and roamed the living area of the suite restlessly. "The thing is, Jack…" She spun around to face him, her luscious backside resting against the desk. "…I know how you feel about not ever marrying again, that you already have your kids."

Knowing where this was going, he concluded grimly, "And that, plus my vasectomy, puts me out of the running for anything permanent or long-lasting, as far as you're concerned."

"It really should."

"It doesn't?"

She came toward him and perched on the edge of the love seat. "After last night? All I want is to be with you again. Which is why I was so jealous tonight, when I saw you with those two women."

He sat knee to knee with her. "They're just colleagues."

"They want to be more than colleagues, Jack."

"Yeah, I got that," he said, glad they had each let down their guard enough to talk about this. "But I'm not interested. I walked them out to the valet and said my goodbye as soon as the taxi got there, so they wouldn't spend more time trying to convince me to go out with them." He set his bottle aside and reached over to take both her hands in his. "When all I really wanted to do was find you and see if we could spend a little more time together tonight. Whether as friends or something more."

Bess perked up. "How about friends with benefits? At least through the holidays?"

Now that she put it like that, Jack thought, a casual relationship wasn't what he wanted from her at all. Fearing they were already limiting their connection way too fast, he reeled her in close and shifted her over onto his lap.

Still, he could take what he could get now and renegotiate for more later. He gave her the agreement she was looking for. "Most definitely through the holidays." He lowered his mouth to hers, felt her lips tremble even as they parted. Connection made, he let himself revel in the taste and feel of her.

And after that, we can reassess, see where things stand.

He sighed his pleasure. Their bodies grew closer, their kiss intensified. "Sounds good to me," he growled.

Her fingers opened the buttons on his shirt. "So... for the immediate future...we're exclusive?"

"Definitely exclusive," he verified.

Bess had never been a particularly sexual person, but Jack made her feel white-hot. All woman. As in need of the emotional comfort and physical satisfaction he was able to give as she was eager to give it in return.

As he continued kissing her hotly, fervently, it no longer seemed like such a risky thing. Yes, they were living in the moment. But as they left their clothes in the living area and moved to the king-size bed, their liaison also seemed inevitable.

Engaging her every sense, he made his way down her body, thoroughly and patiently exploring, indulging every fantasy she had ever had. Shifting from the erotic to the tender and back again, until there only was fierce driving need, only this instant in time as he made her his, and she claimed him in return.

Yielding to him, she trembled as he kissed and caressed her, tracing the petal softness with his fingertips until the moisture flowed. He teased the sensitive insides of her thighs, following with his lips, leaving a path of fire. Switching places, she did the same for him. Tempting and tantalizing, learning anew, until he brought her up to face him, and her hips rose up to meet his as he touched and rubbed and fondled.

Clearly finding her as ready for love as he seemed to be, he slid his hands beneath her and lifted her against him. Her thighs slid open, she met him stroke for stroke, and the warmth of his body gave new heat to hers.

Awash in sensation, her head falling back, she let the abandon overtake her. And then she was moaning, soft and low in her throat, listening to his guttural cry as they tumbled into ecstasy and beyond.

Slowly, they came back to earth. Jack slid a hand down her spine, cuddling her close. "Better?" he asked.

Feeling freer and happier than ever before, she smiled and pressed a kiss against his chest. "Oh, yes." She snuggled against him, loving the way he felt, so strong and solid and male.

It had never been like her to throw caution to the wind like this, never mind open up her heart to someone who she'd known from day one was never going to be able to love her back, at least not the way she wanted.

But when Jack held her and kissed her and made love to her like this, all she could think about was how right he felt pressed up against her. How strong and kind and caring. How understanding and dependable. And she needed that, more than she could even admit, at least for the next few weeks.

So, for once, she decided, as they began to make slow, easy love all over again, she was going to forget trying to figure out if this was all rebound on his part or hers.

And simply enjoy the holidays. With him. And treasure the best present she had ever had.

Chapter Ten

Jack's girls gave him a hero's welcome when he got back from Dallas, and they were still feeling incredibly affectionate when Bess dropped by after dinner to see them, too.

As always, the trio looked adorable, with their tousled blond curls, delicate features, pink cheeks and big blue eyes. They wore matching red-and-white-striped turtlenecks, jeans and colorful Christmas socks and sneakers.

"Bess! Bess! Bess!" they chanted as she walked in the door.

She'd no sooner gotten her coat off and handed it to Jack than they led her to the sofa and settled in close. "Try our cookies, Bess!" Lindsay said. "We made them at Grandma and Grandpa's ranch!"

The rolled sugar cookies were her favorite holiday confection, and these were perfectly imperfect, with their slightly burned edges, unevenly applied butter-cream frosting and overabundance of sprinkles. Clearly, they'd been made with lots and lots of love.

"Daddy ate three!" Chloe reported. "One from each of us!"

"I guess I'll have to keep up, then."

The girls chattered while she munched. "Well, do you like them?" Nicole asked, eager to please as always.

Bess smiled and dabbed the corners of her lips with a napkin. "They are absolutely delicious."

"How about another one for me?" Jack said.

"Just one." Taking charge, Lindsay propped her hands on her hips and warned, "We have to save some for Santa Claus."

Jack looked at the dwindling supply on the plate, seeming as reluctant to ration those as he had been his kisses and caresses. He smiled at his daughters. "That's not for another couple of weeks. Do you really think that there will be any left?"

Three sets of brows furrowed, contemplating the chances of that.

Jack took the opportunity to settle next to Bess on the center of the couch. He draped his arm along the back, as if inviting her to snuggle with him the way she had already snuggled with his girls.

His voice cheerful, he continued, "Don't you think it would be better to put out some fresh new cookies for Santa Claus?"

"We can always make more," Bess said, eager to put any worry to rest.

The girls moved in to drape themselves across Jack's and Bess's laps. In that instant, she had a glimpse of what life might have been like with her and Jack, had he not already had the love of his life.

A trio of faces turned toward her. "Will you help us, Bess? Because we need adult supervision to do stuff in the kitchen. That's the rule."

Too late she realized she should have cleared it with Jack before blurting out her offer. Making love with him hadn't just brought her back to life in the most wonderful of ways, it had lowered the barriers between them. Dangerously so. "If it's okay with your daddy..." she said, aware she may have overstepped.

His eyes twinkled with merriment, telling her she hadn't. "Only if I get to help."

Nicole switched places with Lindsay, eased onto Bess's lap and wreathed her arms around her neck. "Did you write a letter to Santa Claus, Bess?"

She hesitated, feeling like she was about to walk into a minefield. Jack was no help. "No," she explained carefully. "Grown-ups don't really do that."

Chloe frowned. "Then how are you going to get what you want for Christmas?"

Like a gift-wrapped Jack? Bess warned herself to calm down. Be sensible. Remember the fling with Jack was only a fling. "I get presents from my two sisters and two brothers."

The girls sighed their relief. Apparently, they didn't want to think her unhappy any more than their daddy did. "Do you give them presents, too?" Nicole asked.

"Yes, I do."

The girls contemplated that.

"And I'm getting a new puppy, remember?" Bess soothed. She really did not want them to worry about her.

The mention of her new puppy did the trick.

"When does Lady Grace get to come home?" Lindsay asked.

"December 19th."

Chloe took her thumb out of her mouth long enough to ask, "Will we be able to visit her?"

"Yes." Bess smiled. "But we'll have to wait a little bit, till Lady Grace gets acclimated."

Nicole's brows knit together in confusion. "What's... acclimated?"

"Used to being at my house," Bess said, wishing she didn't have to hide anything from the girls, even though she knew it was imperative. "That way it won't be too many changes for her all at once. Because too many changes can scare a puppy." *And a woman my age, too.* "But once she settles in, I promise you all can visit her a lot."

"Can we bring our new puppy that Santa is bringing us?"

"I think having puppy playdates would be a great idea," Bess agreed.

Lindsay grinned. "I know another great idea."

Without warning, there were secret smiles, all around. Indicating something was up. "Do you notice anything different tonight, Daddy?" Nicole asked innocently.

It was Jack's turn to appear as if he were headed into a minefield. "Like what?" he said.

"Like something Christmassy!" Chloe said.

In tandem, all three girls pointed to the light fixture in the adjacent foyer. "Our mistletoe!"

"Our...*what*?" Jack did a double take, as did Bess.

Lindsay slid off Jack's lap. "Grandma helped us hang it when they brought us home and you were outside with Grandpa, getting our stuff out of the car."

Nicole said seriously, "You're supposed to stand beneath it and kiss somebody, Daddy. Like Bess. And, Bess, you're supposed to kiss someone, too. Like Daddy."

Bess did not need to see herself in a mirror to know she had just turned beet red.

Jack followed the girls' line of sight. "Did Grandma tell you that?" he asked, a maddeningly unreadable expression on his handsome face.

Lindsay snorted. "No, silly Daddy! We figured it out all by ourselves. Because people kiss under the mistletoe at Grandma and Grandpa's house *all the time*."

All three girls moved back from the sofa, as if waiting for Bess and Jack to do just that.

It was all Bess could do not to moan aloud.

Jack seemed simply thoughtful and perplexed.

She moved away from him, smiled and, because some response seemed required, said to his three daughters, "Well! That's good to know."

"Going to have a talk with my mother," he muttered so just she could hear.

"Okay." Though knowing Rachel McCabe, Bess wasn't sure it would help. The doting mother of six wanted all her children happily married, and from this blatant matchmaking attempt, it was clear she would do whatever she could to speed things along.

The girls studied the two of them. Finally, Lindsay said to Bess, "Maybe your new puppy will help you find a baby to adopt at the fire station, the way Riot led Aunt Bridgett to baby Robby, and then you can fall in love with a daddy like Aunt Bridgett fell in love with Uncle Cullen, and get married. And then you can get pregnant and have a baby in the hospital, too!"

That was quite the hope, Bess thought.

"Aunt Bridgett has two babies in her tummy," Nicole corrected, a lot less romantically. "Not one."

"She sure does. That's exciting, don't you think?" Bess carried the plate of cookies into the kitchen and set it on the counter. She clapped her hands together. "You know what else is exciting? Taking a walk through the neighborhood to look at the Christmas lights and displays in all the yards!"

"Can we go, Daddy? Can we?"

Jack smiled, relaxing for the first time in several minutes. "Sure."

They all got their coats, hats and gloves and set out, immersing themselves for the next hour in colorful holiday displays.

It worked to distract the girls, but as soon as they returned, they were right back where they had left off. "Daddy!" Lindsay pointed impatiently at the mistletoe in the foyer.

"Kiss her," Chloe hissed.

Jack looked at Bess uncertainly, as aware as she was of giving too much away. "I…"

"Otherwise it's not a merry Christmas," Nicole insisted, jumping up and down. "And we have to have a merry Christmas, don't we, Daddy?"

Seeing no way out of it, Bess lifted her hands in surrender and met Jack's eyes. "When in Rome…"

"But we're not in Rome," Lindsay said, confused.

Jack leaned over and bussed Bess's cheek. "It means taking the path of least resistance," he explained.

They still didn't understand. But they knew one thing, for sure.

"That's not really a kiss, Daddy," Lindsay pointed out.

"Actually," Bess corrected, "it is the perfect kiss." To have in front of watchful little ones, anyway. "Now, who else besides me wants hot chocolate?" She rubbed her hands together and pretended to shiver. "Because I think it's the perfect treat to warm us all up!"

"Sorry about the mistletoe," Jack said an hour and a half later when his girls were finally in bed, sound asleep.

Bess helped him wash up the mugs and the saucepan she'd used to make the hot cocoa. Telling herself she was not the least bit disappointed about the missed opportunity to really lock lips, she waved off his chagrin. "No need. They were just trying to help us get in the spirit of the season."

His shoulder touched hers as he reached over to dry a mug. He winked down at her and said sexily, "I thought we already were."

Still tingling from their accidental contact, she thought back to the two nights they'd shared, and murmured, "Definitely getting there, Doc."

She gazed out the window above the sink, at the starry winter night, and could not help but contrast the cold outside with the warmth she felt in here. She turned to hand him another freshly washed mug. Their fingers brushed briefly, sending another wave of awareness shimmering through her.

"So you really didn't mind all the cheerleading from the girls?"

"Oddly enough, no." She admitted on a wistful sigh, "Their enthusiasm helped remind me that love comes at all times and in all ways."

He transferred the towel to his other hand and tucked a strand of her hair behind her ear. "Well, my girls sure love you," he confessed.

"And I love them, too," she said softly, leaning into his touch.

I love all of you.

Of course she loved her friends and family, and now with Jack… Well, there was no denying that was starting to become something more, she thought as he dropped his hand and stepped back. *A lot more.*

He continued to look down at her, seemingly lost in his own thoughts. Determined to keep her attention away from the tantalizing way they had made love, she focused back on the sink. Pulled out the stopper. Watched as the sudsy water began to drain, and tried not to think just how much she wanted to kiss and make love to him again.

"By the way…" She turned her back to him and moved down the kitchen counter, tidying as she went. "…I don't know if you've had time to check your personal email since we got back from Dallas last night." She put the sugar and cocoa containers away. "Betty Winfield sent out a list of things we're all going to need for our puppies before we take them home."

The oblivious way he looked at her said he had not.

Happy she'd thought to bring it up, she lounged against the opposite counter and continued, "She also reminded everyone to go ahead and make vet appointments for their next set of shots, which should happen a few days after they go home."

To her frustration, Jack's posture was as inscrutable as the expression on his face.

"So…" Suddenly feeling the need to hang on to something, she clasped the Carrara marble edge on either side of her. "I was wondering if you wanted me to save you some time and pick up the puppy stuff for you and store it at my place, or—?"

His eyes crinkled at the corners. "How big is the list?"

She pulled it up on her phone to show him.

He leaned in close to peruse it, inundating her with the familiar scents of soap, bergamot and suede. And heat. So much body heat… "Can we get this stuff in town?"

Bess did her best to control the desire zinging through her. She shrugged and wet her suddenly parched lips. "I'm pretty sure they have everything at the new pet store." She studied her screen with unnecessary intensity, even though she had already long memorized the list.

Noting he had stopped reading and was now studying her, she stepped back. Cleared her throat. "The problem is, if you run into anyone else buying puppy supplies while we are there, it's going to raise questions."

"The kind that I don't want to answer right now."

She nodded, wishing he didn't look so big and strong and handsome. "And the girls could get wind of your plans inadvertently. But on the other hand—" she angled her thumb at the center of her chest "—everyone already knows I'm going to get a new puppy, so if I were to go alone and pick up what we both need, it wouldn't be quite as attention-getting or worthy of gossip."

As would be the news of the two of them hooking up.

His gaze drifted down to her hand and back up again. "Except for the fact you'd be buying two of everything," he pointed out.

"I'd just say I was getting extra stuff for when we visit my family's Triple Canyon Ranch."

Aware he was gauging her actions as carefully as she was checking out his, she inhaled and breathed out slowly. Lifted her chin. "So, as I said, if you want me to do it, I'd be happy to go solo. We can settle up later."

Jack knew what Bess was suggesting was practical. The trouble was, if she did it alone, he would miss out on a prime opportunity to spend more time with her. And with Christmas now two weeks away, and their deal set to end soon after, he did not want to waste any chances to be close to her. "Actually, I'd like to be part of that. So how about we go together?"

She looked up at him. She wasn't easy to read, now that she had her guard up again.

"Are you sure?" Her bright smile looked forced. "It's no trouble, really."

"I figure if I'm going to be a dog owner, I need to learn a lot more about this stuff," he fibbed, inhaling her sweet womanly fragrance. "So how about we go to San Angelo?" Half an hour away, there was much less chance of running into prying eyes. Which meant he could let down *his* guard and flirt with her. In public.

She paused to look at her phone again, scrolling through information about pet stores in San Angelo. "Looks like there are two shops, and both of them have holiday hours. And will stay open until 10:00 p m."

"Well, that's great news." He followed her through the hall to the foyer. She slid her phone into her bag and he helped her on with her coat, pulling her hair from the collar.

She turned to face him, blushing slightly.

Reluctant to stop touching her, he let his hand linger at the nape of her neck. "Are you free tomorrow evening?" He adjusted his posture to ease the pressure at the front of his jeans. "Say around seven o'clock?"

"I will be." She paused. "The vet checkup may be a little harder to arrange for your puppy. Since you can't be seen going out of the vet clinic with an adorable golden in tow."

Jack chuckled, knowing this to be true. "This is where having your brother engaged to a veterinarian comes in handy. I'll find out if Sara Anderson can either do an after-hours house call for both of our puppies simultaneously, or allow us to take the pups out to her ranch for their first checkup."

"That would be great."

He thought so, too. She moved as if to collect her bag. Not about to let her go without a proper goodbye, he intercepted her midreach, clasped her shoulders and steered her gently under the mistletoe.

She drew a quick breath. "What are you doing?"

Like she didn't know. Jack cupped her face between his hands and tilted his head to just the right angle. "Making up for earlier," he murmured, touching his lips to first one corner of her mouth, then the other. "With a proper kiss."

Her mouth opened in a round O of surprise, and he settled in the middle of her sweet, succulent lips, holding her still while he took full possession. Knowing that no matter how long or slow or thoroughly he kissed her that he would never get enough. Bess was everything he had ever wanted in a woman. Engendering the kind of happiness he'd figured he'd never have again. It was more than friendship, more than sex. Something stronger and far more life-altering. He was reveling in it, and he could tell she was, too.

Which was why it was imperative one of them come to their senses. She drew back. "The girls…" Her voice trembled as much as the rest of her.

"I know. This is going to have to hold us," he whispered playfully, wishing he could follow her back to her house and make love to her. But with Mrs. D. not set to return until early the following morning to care for his girls, their lovemaking would have to wait.

But not for long. Not if he had anything to do with it. Because if there was anything the past few weeks had taught him, it was that he didn't want Bess exiting his life to find love and build a family elsewhere.

Maybe it was selfish, considering all he still could not give her, but he wanted her for himself.

Chapter Eleven

Monday evening, Jack picked Bess up as previously planned. A cold front had come in during the afternoon, and the temperature hovered just above freezing. As she got into his SUV, she turned to him and said, "I hope you don't mind, but I sort of…um…started without you."

He chuckled as he slid behind the wheel and started the engine. Noticing she was shivering, he turned up the heater and slanted her a playful glance. "Hmm." He drew out the sound until it carried a wealth of meaning. "Sounds…interesting."

His clowning around earned him an eye roll and a laugh. "Maybe not as much as you think," she quipped, flirting a little bit, too.

She was wearing an ivory turtleneck sweater beneath a fitted black fleece jacket. Snug-fitting green cords and fancy black Western boots with multicolored scrolling completed her ensemble. And she'd put on some earrings and had done something with her hair that made her look sexy as hell.

All he wanted to do was take her in his arms and kiss her until they lost all track of time and place, and then go inside her house and make love to her again. But the time crunch they were facing had him obediently backing out of her driveway.

He cleared his throat and willed his overheated body to cool down. "So, what've you been up to?"

She settled in her seat. "I did a little online Christmas shopping after I left your place last night. And I found these glow-in-the-dark canvas collars, harnesses and leashes that could also be embroidered with the dog's name and emergency contact number."

Although they both planned to have their dogs microchipped, that could not be done until they were a little older. "Sounds like a great thing to have."

Her smile was filled with the Christmas spirit that had been lacking a few weeks before. "I know, right?"

"Always better to be safe than sorry," he said, reaching over and briefly squeezing her hand.

Bess looked down at their entwined palms, before gazing back up at him. "Anyway, I went ahead and ordered them for both puppies," she confessed, her silky skin warming beneath his. "Pink for Princess Abigayle, because I know that is one of the girls' favorite colors, and rose for Lady Grace."

She paused, her brow furrowing. "I hope that's not too presumptuous." As she straightened in her seat, she withdrew her hand. "I mean, I could have called you, but it was after midnight, and if I didn't get them ordered pronto, they weren't going to be guaranteed to arrive before Christmas." She released an anxious sigh. "At least not with the embroidered information. So I went ahead and did it."

"Sounds great. Thank you." He promised to settle up with her later, then asked, "Are they being shipped to your place or mine or both?"

Bess wrinkled her nose in that cute way he loved. "Actually, it's an item that's going to have to be signed for. So I'm having them sent to Monroe's Western Wear. The store can sign for them, and my brother Nick will hold them for me. I'll get them to you from there."

Impressed, he said, "The girls will be so excited."

"I think so, too."

The Christmas music on the radio played softly in the background. She turned to him as he stopped at a red light at the edge of San Angelo. "You really don't mind?" she asked tentatively.

He shook his head. "I appreciate everything you do for us. Don't you know that by now?" He clasped her hand and lifted it to his lips. Then, unable to help himself, he kissed the inside of her wrist. "But for the record, you can always call me." His eyes lasered into hers. "No matter what time of day or night it is."

Bess blushed. "I wasn't going to wake you for something that inconsequential."

The traffic light turned green. Jack dropped his hold on her and drove on. "First of all," he said, paying attention to the street signs, "if it's important to you—or the girls—it's never inconsequential. Second..." He saw the shopping center they were looking for and turned onto Sunset Drive. "...I just want to make the point that I'm here for you. Whenever, however, you need me."

Bess flashed him a grateful look. "Thank you. And as long as we're making points, Doc," she added, "I'm there for you, too."

"As you have proven many, many times."

In fact, he didn't know what he and the girls would have done without her the past few years. He swallowed around the sudden lump in his throat. "Now, which store are we hitting first?"

Abruptly looking a little emotional, too, Bess directed him to the larger of the two.

Which turned out to be a good choice. It was well stocked with everything they could need. In short order, they picked out food and water dishes, the kibble the puppies were currently eating at the breeders', and the extra collars and leashes they would need in the days leading up to Christmas. Then there were the piddle pads and pet stain remover for carpet and hardwood floors, puppy shampoo, chew toys and bones. Soon their cart was overflowing.

Jack moved over to let someone else pass through the aisle. "What do we have left?" he asked as his body briefly pressed against hers.

Bess was having trouble concentrating.

Maybe it was the way they were going somewhere together in the evening, in a way that felt like a date, even though she knew darn well it wasn't a date, any more than their shopping trip over the weekend for dollhouses and baby dolls had been a date.

And maybe it was the way he had kissed her beneath the mistletoe the previous evening, in a way that had left her wanting more...

All she knew for certain was that Jack looked incredibly handsome in the gray suede jacket worn with a blue button-down and jeans that brought out the cobalt blue of his eyes.

"Um..." She tried to focus on his question. Still tingling all over from where they had pressed up against each other, she checked her list. "Crates. Betty suggested we get a small plastic travel crate for the ride home for each of them, and then a large wire crate with a divider for use at home."

"Why a divider?" Jack asked as he pushed the cart toward the crates.

She fell into step beside him. "Apparently, if the sleeping space is too big, it causes issues." When he looked down at her, she explained, "If you have a divider, you can make their resting space as small and cozy as they need, then enlarge the space gradually as they grow, until you take the divider out altogether."

His eyes crinkled at the corners. "Sounds reasonable."

Unfortunately, there was only one extra-large-size metal crate, suitable for full-grown dogs, on display. While Jack flagged down an employee to check for another, Bess perused the nearby sleeping cushions.

Jack returned just as her phone signaled an incoming message. She checked the screen. "Oh, wow, poor guy," she murmured with a heartfelt sigh.

He quirked his brow.

She shook her head sympathetically. "Tim Briscoe is on a date I set up for him tonight. It's with one of the teachers at the preschool. I thought they'd really hit it off, but he says it's going badly."

Jack did a double take. "He's on the date right now?"

"Yes."

His irritation plain, he scoffed. "Well, no wonder it's going badly if he's texting you while he's sitting there with another woman."

Surprised the normally easygoing Jack was being so judgmental, Bess scowled and continued looking at her phone. "She went to the powder room." She glanced back up at him. "He wants to know if I have any suggestions about how to liven things up."

He shrugged his broad shoulders. "He could get a clue. Seriously, don't you think you're a little too involved with all this?"

Bess censured him with a narrow-eyed look. "No," she said.

The clerk came back, all smiles. "You're in luck!" she sang out. "We've got one more left. So when you're done shopping and check out, I'll bring both around to the front and help put them in your vehicle."

"Thank you," Jack said. "We appreciate your help."

What he clearly did not appreciate was her friendship with Tim.

"What else do we need to get?" he asked impatiently.

Bess had had her eye on a comfy dog cushion to put in her living room, but she knew she could get that at the pet store in Laramie. Deciding she and Jack were getting a little too irritated with each other, she said, "This is it."

Jack seemed to know he had stepped over a line. "Sure?"

She nodded as another text came in. This time she did not tell Jack it was Tim, this time asking if he should go ahead and end the date early to put them both out of their misery or keep trying. She typed in a suggestion that they walk over to the town square and admire the decorations in the park before calling a halt to the date. Then she switched the sound off and put her cell phone away.

They went to the registers and paid, their earlier lighthearted mood gone. "I'll wait here with the cart while you get your SUV," Bess said stiffly.

Jack nodded and headed off. By the time he had returned and put the rear seats flat, the clerk had come out with the dolly. The crates were bulky and heavy and were loaded in first. Everything else they'd purchased was situated on top.

"Anything else you want to do while we're here?" Jack asked, his earlier pique with her clearly gone.

Unable to let her own annoyance with him go as easily, Bess shook her head. "I think we're all set. I'd really like to go home."

"How long are you going to stay ticked at me?" Jack asked, when they'd arrived at her house and finished unloading all their purchases.

"I'm not ticked off."

He put his hands lightly on her shoulders, then bent down so he could see into her face. "Yeah. You are."

She planted her hand on the center of his chest and pushed him away, then gave him a withering look. "Okay. If you really want to go there…"

It was apparent that she didn't.

He let his gaze drift over her pouting lips and the fire of resentment in her eyes. "I really do." Whether she liked it or not, they were going to get their feelings out in the open. He wasn't about to let their relationship fall into the pattern of his former marriage—whenever he had displeased Gayle, he'd get the silent treatment for days on end.

Angling her chin up at him, she asked angrily, "Where do you get off telling me who I can and cannot advise on their love life?"

Knowing he wasn't the one at fault here, he looked at her for a long moment. "Is that what you think you were doing tonight when you were texting with Tim?"

She moved past him with a glare, picked up the

smaller packages they had just brought in and put them into a mostly empty supply closet. She whirled back to him and leaned up against the door, hands braced behind her. "Yes. I was helping out a friend."

Sensing she needed her physical space, he leaned against the opposite wall and folded his arms in front of him. He clarified, "A friend who'd rather be on a date with you than the woman he was with tonight."

"That's not true."

Jack wished he could just kiss her again, without driving her further away than she was at this very moment, and end this silly argument. Knowing, however, that nothing would be solved by pretending there wasn't a problem, he noted the way her breasts were rising and falling with each breath. With effort, he returned his gaze to her face. "Trust me on this, Bess. If Tim didn't still have a thing for you—" a fact Jack could easily comprehend, given how sexy and kind she was "—Tim wouldn't have been texting you for advice."

Stiffening, she pushed away from the wall, letting her hands fall to her sides. "Trust me on this. Tim is not still interested in me like that."

Jack pushed away from the wall, too, unsure whether she was being naive or he was overreacting out of pure male jealousy. "Sure about that?"

"Positive." Closing the distance between them, she pressed her index finger against the center of his chest. "What I am not so sure about is why *you* are acting as if you and I were on a date tonight and Tim interrupted it."

"You really don't know?" Jack deadpanned.

"No. I really don't!"

Every territorial part of him went into overdrive. The truth was, he couldn't stand the thought of her with another man. Because she belonged with him now.

"Well, maybe…" he growled, wrapping one arm around her waist and sifting the other through her hair. He tilted his head over hers, then slowly and deliberately lowered his mouth. "…this will show you."

Bess had plenty of time to step away. Call a halt. But apparently she didn't want to prevent this kiss. Any more than she wanted the evening to end without the two of them making hot, wild, passionate love again.

His mouth captured hers in a sweet and mesmerizing kiss that encouraged her to answer his kiss with her own. And she did. Rising on tiptoe, looping her arms about his neck, she savored the warmth and solid strength of him. Their passion intensified as he brought her closer still, wrapping her tight in his arms. Sighing rapturously, her lips parted beneath the pressure of his as his tongue swept the inside of her mouth with long, deliberate strokes.

He backed her against the washer and parted her knees with his thigh. She trembled all the more, and still they kissed, taking a sensual tour of each other's lips, revealing to each other everything it would have been so much safer to deny.

His hands eased beneath her ivory turtleneck. "We've both got on way too many clothes," he murmured, making her laugh.

"Well." She kissed his shoulder. "There is a solution for that."

He grinned. "Glad you suggested that."

The next thing she knew, he had lifted her onto the washing machine.

"Not the bedroom?" she teased, as he knelt before her, tugging off one fancy Western boot, then the other.

"Too far."

She expected him to rise, but he stayed where he was. Handsome head nestled between her knees.

She'd never viewed herself as an impatient person. But that was changing. Fast. She stroked her fingers through his hair. "I need you up here," she whimpered.

He stayed where he was, kissing his way up the insides of her knees and thighs.

Another lightning bolt of desire swept through her. She yanked off her turtleneck, let it flutter onto his shoulders. Her bra hit his head.

It was his turn to laugh. "Messaging me?" He rose, slowly, deliberately.

She wrinkled her nose. "Something like that."

"Ah, well, then." He reached for the zipper on her cords. "Let's see if you match."

She lifted slightly so he could ease the fabric down, past her hips, over her thighs and knees. He stepped back to view the satin bikini panties that matched her discarded bra. "Oh, yeah." He waved the bra like a victory flag, then stepped in again, parting her thighs, pulling her to the edge of the washer. She quivered as his hands cupped her breasts, rubbing her already sensitive nipples into aching buds.

Lower still, moisture reigned.

She unbuttoned his shirt, spread the fabric wide. He unzipped and stepped out of his jeans. And still they kissed endlessly until what few boundaries yet between them dissolved. She wrapped her legs snugly around his waist as he dropped kisses at her temple, the delicate shell of her ear, the pulse in her throat.

Lowering his head, he flicked the tip of her breast with his tongue, while his other hand dipped lower, slipping beneath the waistband of her panties. An exultant cry escaped her as his fingers led the way and found a rhythm that left her shuddering. Needing. Pleading.

He penetrated her slowly, then moved deeper still. She hung on to him, rocked up against him, as he tilted her in a way that pleased them both. Seduced her. Encouraged her to take him even more tightly inside her.

Afterward, they clung together, still shuddering with pleasure. Bess rested her head on his shoulder, still trying to catch her breath.

Talk about amazing!

"I'll never do laundry the same way again," she whispered. Just the act of entering the door and stepping inside the utility room would bring back memories of this sizzling-hot encounter.

Jack let out a belly laugh every bit as sexy as he was. "Me neither…" He hooked her legs around his waist and slid her off the washer, so her lower body was pressed against him.

Once again, Bess found it difficult to resist him. Excitement roared through her. "What are you doing?"

Jack laughed again and playfully nuzzled her neck, before ravishing her lips. "Taking you to bed for round two…"

Hours later, Bess woke, her body still humming with satisfaction. The pillow beside her was empty except for a single piece of paper. She reached for the handwritten message as eagerly as she would have reached for him.

It said simply, *Sleep tight… Jack.*

Not exactly a love note.

But given the fact they were simply enjoying a temporary holiday fling…probably appropriate.

Shaking off a sudden burst of melancholy, she slid the note into the drawer in her bedside table for safekeeping. So he hadn't signed it *love*, or even left any *X*s and *O*s. So what? She couldn't ask Jack to behave like a boyfriend, because they weren't a regular couple. And they weren't going to be, thanks to the very adult and pragmatic agreement they had made.

But—the corners of her lips curved up as she recalled just how thoroughly he had made love to her that evening—that didn't mean she couldn't milk the next few weeks for all they were worth.

Aware it was almost time to go to work anyway, Bess rose and hit the shower. Her phone rang just as she was getting out.

Despite her internal lecture about playing it cool, the name on the caller ID sent her heart into overdrive. She picked up. "Hey," she said.

"Hey," Jack said back, his voice sweet and tender. "I didn't know if you had preset your alarm or not, but thought I'd call in case you hadn't."

So he *had* been thinking of her.

Just as she had been thinking of him.

"I'm up," she told him softly, "but…thanks." For calling. For caring, at least this much.

"Bess?"

"Hmm?"

"One more thing."

"Yes?" she asked with bated breath.

His voice dropped another sexy notch. "Last night was spectacular."

A shiver of pleasure sifting through her, Bess held the phone a little closer to her ear. "For me, too."

Chapter Twelve

"You look happy," Bridgett said at the conclusion of the surprise baby shower in her honor late that same day.

"And yet you're the one who is on maternity leave, as of—" Bess glanced at her watch "—one hour ago."

NICU colleagues had gathered in the staff break room both before and at the end of their shift to inundate Bess's twin with gifts and wish her well on her maternity leave. Bess had left the rehab unit a little early, in order to join them.

Bridgett ran a hand over her swollen tummy. "Yeah, it's going to be weird not coming to work with the preemies a couple of times a week for an entire year."

Bess understood. Although they'd gone into different specialties, she and her sister both shared a love of nursing that went back to their time as teen volunteers. She sat down next to Bridgett on the sofa. "You know you can sub as needed, and Cullen and I will both help out with Robby and the twins when you do come in to the hospital. It's all good, sis."

Bridgett paused. "You really think I'm going to be able to handle all this?"

"I know so." Bess hugged her very pregnant sister as best she could. She offered a reassuring smile. "How could you not with both the McCabe and the Monroe clans nearby, all standing ready to help you out?"

"True." With a sigh, Bridgett levered herself up and off her chair. With all the guests gone, it was time to clean up. The cake, punch and assorted tea sandwiches were being left for the on-duty personnel, but the gifts had to be loaded onto a cart.

"But back to you." Bridgett smiled. "Generally speaking, the closer we get to Christmas, the grouchier you are. This year, it seems the opposite."

Bess put discarded wrapping paper into the trash. "I guess that's what happens when you write two Christmas letters, one ridiculously happy and one ridiculously sad. You end up being forced to find middle ground."

Bridgett put a breast pump onto the cart. "Except this isn't middle ground. This is all-out happy."

Because of Jack, Bess thought. And all the time she was spending with him and the girls. "It's probably because I'm looking forward to my new puppy."

Bridgett scoffed. "Not even a new puppy could put a glow like that in your cheeks. Seriously. What is going on with you? Did you decide to give Tim another chance or something? I heard he was going on a date last night."

"No. Tim's date was with someone else. He and I are just friends."

"Is it Jack?"

Bess tensed. She had a feeling her family would not

approve of the bargain she had struck with the sexy surgeon. "What do you mean?" she asked as innocently as possible.

Bridgett stacked layette items. "Well, I can't ever get ahold of you. Cullen and Chase and Matt and Dan can't get ahold of Jack. It's beginning to look to some of us, anyway, that the two things might be related."

"Why would they all be calling Jack?" Unless they, too, wanted to pry.

Bridgett tidied up the buffet. "Well, they are all brothers."

Which told her exactly nothing, Bess thought. She edged closer. "I'm serious, Bridgett." Was something up? Had Jack's brothers figured out she and Jack were now lovers, as well as friends? She was pretty sure he would not have told them anything about their fling. Like her, he liked to keep his private life very private. Then again, since the weekend in Dallas, Jack had been looking awfully cheerful, too. "Why are his brothers all suddenly trying to get ahold of Jack?"

Apparently realizing she'd inadvertently worried Bess, Bridgett sobered. "There's a McCabe family get-together after the preschool holiday sing-along this week on Thursday evening, at Kelly and Dan's house."

Kelly was a teacher at the preschool and mother to four-year-old triplets. Resolutely single after a failed marriage, she had nevertheless fallen in love with and married Jack's deputy sheriff brother, Dan, the year before.

"It won't be long, it being a school night and all. We just want to provide pizza and ice cream for the kids. We all thought since you'll probably be going to see your nieces and nephews, and Jack and the girls are definitely going to be there, you might want to come over afterward, too."

That made sense. And normally, Bess would be happy to be included in a McCabe family gathering, as she had been many times before, even before Bridgett had married Jack's brother Cullen.

Now, well, things were a little bit different. She didn't want to presume anything and just show up, for fear it would upset the delicate balance of their fling. "Isn't it usually up to Jack to ask if he wants my company?"

"Yes." Her twin regarded her steadily. "But like we said—" she flashed a merry smile "—none of us can seem to get ahold of either of you, so. . ." She held out her hands, as if jumping to the next logical conclusion.

"Not you, too," Bess accused her sister dryly. She should have known she wouldn't be able to keep anything from her twin.

Bridgett widened her eyes. "What?"

"Matchmaking for me and Jack? When just a few weeks ago you and the rest of our siblings were warning me away from him."

"Maybe that was a mistake," Bridgett conceded frankly.

Bess swallowed. "What makes you think that?"

"How truly happy you suddenly are. Him, too."

Bess knew that was true. Yet having the change in their relationship out in the open suddenly made her feel ambivalent all over again. As if their joy were too good to last. Past the holidays, anyway. "You know as well as I do that he already had the love of his life." And didn't want another marriage. Or more kids. She had to keep remembering that.

"So what are you saying, that it's a no go because you haven't had yours?"

Bess hid her discomfort. Her sister knew better than anyone how she had hated playing second fiddle to the past loves of her previous boyfriends. How being in a rebound relationship only led to heartache.

"I'll get what I want in that regard eventually." And even if she didn't ever find her one true love, the way Jack had, she was pretty happy now. So was Jack. That had to count for something, didn't it?

Bridgett paused. "Maybe it's time you did more than just trust fate to make it happen for you."

"The way it did for you and Cullen?"

"Yes. Robby and Riot might have brought us together, but there is no reason why you have to wait around for something similar to happen, sis."

Bess didn't think she should expect an abandoned baby and a puppy to show up at a fire station the way they had for Bridgett. She swallowed around the uncertainty building inside her. "What are you advising me to do?" she asked quietly.

Bridgett squeezed her hand. "I want you to take the leap and go for whatever this is that's been developing between you and Jack for some time now. Or move on, the way we all advised you to do when we thought… erroneously, it seems…that your attraction to Jack was destined to go unrealized. Although I personally think you should give love the chance it deserves."

"Oh my god!" Bess clapped a hand to her forehead. Talk about familial pressure! "Now I'm back to thinking I will never get through this season."

Bridgett grinned, unrepentant. She reached for her coat and bag. "Someone else matchmaking now, too?" she teased.

Bess nodded reluctantly and looped her cross-body bag over her shoulder. "Rachel and Frank installed mistletoe in Jack's foyer while we were in Dallas last weekend."

This time her sister laughed out loud. "Great minds think alike." She looked behind Bess, then whispered, "And speaking of the sexy surgeon…"

Bess turned.

There he was, looking handsome as ever in the blue scrubs that emphasized the muscles of his tall, fit frame. "Stop!" Bess hissed.

Looking as confident and masculine as ever, Jack strolled up. He read their faces. "Problem here, ladies?"

"Yes." To Bess's distress, her twin was quick to jump in and play the pregnant damsel in distress. "We were wondering how we were going to push this very heavy cart all the way out to the parking lot."

Bess was not about to put Jack on the spot like that. She lifted a palm. "I've got it."

"No need. I'm here and happy to help." He stepped behind the cart and began to push it through the doorway. Bess and Bridgett followed him down the hall, toward the service elevator. "Looks like you and Cullen really made out in the gift department."

Bridgett beamed her gratitude. "We did."

Talk turned to the baby shower. Bess made sure it stayed there, until they finally made it downstairs and exited the hospital lobby. Jack brought Bridgett's minivan around from the parking lot, and then he and Bess worked together to load up the gifts while Bridgett eased behind the wheel.

"Thanks for helping," Bess said, shutting the tailgate. He had made the task go a lot faster.

Bridgett put the passenger window down and leaned toward them. "Want me to give you a ride to your cars?"

Jack lifted a brow and looked at Bess. She could tell

he wanted to talk to her about something. Whatever it was, she had no intention of letting her twin eavesdrop. "It's not necessary," she said, doing her best to hold back a guilty conscience.

"I guess not," Bridgett teased. "Behave yourselves, you two. And don't forget to ask him about Thursday!" She waved and drove away.

Jack walked with Bess to take the cart back into the hospital. "What's Thursday?"

A passing orderly reached for the cart. "I've got it," he said. They thanked him as he took it away, and they walked back outside.

"The preschool holiday sing-along," Bess said at last.

Jack's eyes lit up with anticipation. "The girls are really excited about it. They've been wanting me to ask if you'd go to see them."

"I know. They already asked me to go the last time I saw them, and I said I would try to be there for either the performance or the dress rehearsal at the school earlier in the day, which Mrs. D. is planning to attend."

His brow furrowed. "So what's the problem?"

"There's a McCabe family gathering afterward, Thursday evening, at Kelly and Dan's." The kind of thing where plus-ones were always welcome and everyone showed up with some sort of food or beverage contribution in hand. "Apparently, I've been invited by the rest of your family. And Bridgett wants me to go to that, as well."

Jack gave her the kind of look that said he wanted nothing more than to kiss her again. He edged closer. "So do I, actually," he said casually.

Bess had figured, but...

Ignoring the telltale fluttering in her midriff, she said, "I'm not so sure that's a good idea."

* * *

This was new, Jack thought. Usually Dess leaped at the chance to attend his family gatherings. And she'd been to quite a few with him, since potlucks were held at either his parents' home or his or one of his five siblings' nearly every week.

"Why not?"

She exhaled and looked up at him. "Because I'm afraid if people see us together, they'll know something has changed."

"You're afraid they'll figure out we've been sleeping together."

A furrow formed between her eyebrows. "Aren't you?"

"I'm not ashamed that we've made love, no," he observed, while she peered up at him through a fringe of dark lashes. "But you are."

"I just..." She struggled. Finally swallowed and said, "I like things the way they are, Jack."

So did he—if she meant spending time together and making love. Except he wanted more. Much more than he had expected. "Understood," he said. One thing was clear. He was going to have to work harder, if he didn't want this to end when they had originally said it would. "So what are your plans for tonight?"

She looked surprised by the abrupt change of subject. "I've got a couple of tickets to the nine o'clock showing of *It's a Wonderful Life*."

Their eyes met and he felt the connection between them deepen. "That's a remake, isn't it?"

"Yep. Starring Bradley Cooper and it's supposed to be good."

He let his gaze rove her face. "Who are you going with?"

Her smile widened. "No one. Yet. The tickets were a gift."

"In response to your two Christmas letters?"

"You got it." Her lips twisted thoughtfully. "Anyway, I wasn't sure I was going to use them—"

"Hey." He palmed the center of his chest facetiously. "I'd love to go."

She let out a flirtatious laugh. "I didn't ask."

"I know." Boy, did he ever! He peered at her closely. "But in case you were thinking of it," he added helpfully.

She studied him, then teased, "Wrangling for a date, Doc?"

"And I'm not too shy to admit it. So what do you say? You supply the tickets. I'll buy the concessions. And I'll pick you up at eight thirty." That would give him time to have dinner with his girls and put them to bed before leaving them in Mrs. D.'s capable care.

Bess hesitated.

Why, he didn't know. "Going once. Going twice…"

"Okay." She lifted her hands in surrender. "I'll see you then."

He smiled. Victory at last. They were both still at work, so kissing her would have to be tabled until later. But he leaned down to whisper in her ear. "Can't wait."

"Is it me?" Bess whispered, as she and Jack settled into their seats midway up the theater. She gave in to a full body shiver. "Or is it cold in here?"

"Definitely cold." Jack set the popcorn bucket and boxes of chocolate caramel candy in the empty seat to his left.

She set their two sodas in the drink holders to their right. They stood, facing each other. Excitement rip-

CATHY GILLEN THACKER 143

pled through her. Because it was the late show on a weeknight, the theater was near empty. "I don't know whether to take off my coat or not," she said.

He studied the vents overhead. "Feels like they've got the heat going now. Maybe they had it off earlier to save energy."

"Makes sense." Especially because their local multiplex wasn't open during the day, except for Saturdays and Sundays. She undid the snaps on her parka. "I guess I'll take mine off."

He guided it off her shoulders.

Her pulse racing at the prospect of sitting next to him in the dark, she draped it against the back of her seat. "I can still put it around me if I need to."

He took his jacket off, too. Leaned down close enough to buss her temple. "Or you could just snuggle up to me." He winked. "Then we'd both be warm."

More than that, she thought. Another tingle of awareness swept through her. Their fingers brushed as she handed him his drink. "Behave yourself, Dr. McCabe."

He looked pained. "Tall order, Nurse Monroe."

She couldn't help it. In public or not, she returned his mischievous grin. A lighthearted vibe shimmered between them. Deciding she may as well enjoy this experience to the hilt, because who knew if they would ever end up at the movies alone again, she turned toward him, so her knee pressed against his thigh.

The scent of the hot, freshly popped corn and rich chocolate tantalized them both. "So…" she murmured. "How would you feel about dumping the box of candy into the bucket?"

Pleasure engulfed his smile. "You do that, too?" He held the bucket while she added the candy.

"Every chance I get," she admitted. "Makes for sweet and salty goodness."

He whispered in her ear. "I know what else makes for sweet and salty goodness."

She grinned. The lights dimmed and the trailers for coming attractions began. A few more couples, along with some lone individuals, made their way in, finding seats in the dark.

Earlier, Bess had worried who they might run into. Now all she could think about was how right it felt to be there with Jack, sitting so close they touched. And how much fun she was having already.

The movie began, and soon they were completely caught up in the reimagined *It's a Wonderful Life*. The updated Frank Capra classic could have been the depiction of her life the previous month. Not nearly so tragic in actual events, of course, but the emotions depicted, the sense of hopelessness and despair of ever getting her life where she wanted it to be, were spot-on. As was the appearance of the angel…or in other words, her Jack… coming in to save the day.

When the joyous denouement arrived, tears of happiness and relief were streaming down her face. Bess looked for a tissue. Only to have several thrust into her hand.

"Figured you would need these," Jack teased.

She looked up at him, as the credits rolled and the lights slowly increased. "Uh-huh." She tracked the moisture beneath his eyelid with her fingertip. "Seems I'm not the only one."

"What can I say?" He leaned over to touch noses with her. "I'm a big old softy in here." He touched the center of his chest.

A throat cleared from the aisleway. "I can second that," a familiar male voice said.

They turned in unison. Jack's brother Chase was standing there with his wife, Mitzy. "Looks pretty cozy here," Chase drawled.

"Chase..." Mitzy warned.

He shrugged. "Just saying."

Jack stood, helped Bess to her feet, then reached over and shook his brother's hand. He leaned in to give his sister-in-law a hug. "Shouldn't you two be home with your quadruplets?"

Nice change of subject, Bess thought, relieved.

Chase grinned. "Mitzy's mom and stepdad are in town. They insisted we have a night out alone. Although..."

Mitzy picked up where her husband left off. "We figured four toddlers at bedtime might be too much, so we stayed to get them tucked in before we headed out."

Bess smiled. "How are the boys?" she asked.

"Great. Active. Well..." She looked at her husband with a veteran social worker's tact. "...we should probably be going, cowboy."

Chase got the hint. He winked. "Nice to see you two together like this. Finally."

Mitzy murmured another warning and eased him away.

"Sorry about that," Bess said as she put on her coat and began gathering up their things.

"I'm not," Jack said, giving her an ornery grin.

"Assumptions were made," she said, her emotions suddenly all fired up.

He gave her waist a playful squeeze before letting her go. "Assumptions never bother me." But there was nothing detached about the look on his handsome face. "What does nag at me a little bit is when I forget something. Like what I wanted to have already asked you tonight."

"And what would that be?"

He reached over to straighten the hood of her parka, untangling it from the ends of her hair. "To come over to my house tomorrow night and decorate gingerbread houses with the girls and me."

Bess felt suddenly much closer to her goal of husband and kids. Warning herself not to assume too much too fast, she asked, "Isn't that sort of a private family activity?"

"It is." Jack lifted his hand to her face and rubbed his thumb over her cheekbone, then down the curve of her lower lip. His eyes darkened before he dropped his palm. "And it's about time you were included," he told her huskily. "Plus, the girls really want you to come."

Realizing this was mostly the girls' doing, Bess's wariness faded. "Okay, then, sure," she said with a matter-of-fact smile. "What do I need to bring?"

Jack took their trash in one hand, slid his other palm beneath her elbow and guided her down the stairs of the now empty theater. "Just yourself," he advised, "and a whole lot of patience and artistic creativity."

It was eleven thirty when Jack parked in the driveway of Bess's home. She had left the holiday lights on that framed her porch and the front of her house. A small tabletop tree lit up the dining room window. It made a festive and yet somehow lonely picture. Good in that she was now celebrating the holiday with the vigor she should, but sad, too, like she was still getting only a small portion of the happiness she deserved.

She'd been quiet on the short ride home from the theater. He wasn't sure what she'd been thinking about. The underlying sadness through most of the movie, before the joyous ending? Running into his brother and sister-in-law?

He only knew that whatever it was had left her feeling vulnerable in a way he really hated to see.

Her eyes locked on his. Without warning, her emotional guard was back up. "Thank you for coming with me tonight, but you're off duty now. You don't have to walk me in."

Like he was going to let the chance to kiss her properly good-night go by? When this was the closest thing they'd ever had to an actual date?

Jack scoffed. "Bah humbug, woman! Of course I do." He was already out of the car, coming around to get her door before she could take her seat belt off. "I was raised a Texas gentleman, remember?" He gave her a hand out of his SUV, then escorted her up the walk. "My mama would have my hide if she knew I left a lady standing in the driveway."

Laughing, Bess slid her key in the lock and opened the front door. Stood in the threshold, blocking his way. "Well, it was awfully nice of you, Jack, but I think in our case Rachel would understand if you had made a quick getaway. Especially given how late it is."

Jack doubted that. Not that his parents' view of his love life or previous lack thereof was any concern to him.

"Neither here nor there," he said lightly. "And I'm happy to note, the clock hasn't struck midnight yet. So... what do you say? Going to invite me in for eggnog?"

She threw back her head and laughed again, and it was a lovely, soft musical sound. "You don't like eggnog."

Not dissuaded in the least, he mimicked a very proper British accent. "A spot of tea, then?"

She burst into giggles again, and Jack knew he had her. "Fine." Still chuckling, she lifted a hand in airy surrender, then took him by the wrist and guided him into the house, shutting the door behind them. After their coats and her bag found their way into a chair, she shook her head. "I don't know how you could possibly hold anything after all that popcorn and candy and diet soda we had, but sure… I'll put on a kettle if it will make you happy."

He admired the sway of her hips beneath her trim black slacks and the way her fitted blouse clung to her breasts, as she led the way into the kitchen. It took every ounce of his self-restraint to keep his thoughts to himself.

"You have to enjoy your last few days of solitude," he said. "After that, it'll be puppy chaos all the time."

There'd be no more completely carefree evenings. No more getting to know each other the way they needed to if they were to take whatever this was turning out to be to the next level.

She smiled at him, and he lounged against the counter across from her, his arms braced on either side of him. Powerful chemistry arced between them.

"What do you know about puppy chaos?" she countered.

"Not nearly enough, I imagine," he murmured, distracted by the upward tilt of her lips and the tousled waves of her hair.

She sashayed closer and splayed her hands across his chest. Mischief glimmering in her eyes, she looked up at him, as if quietly contemplating their options for what was left of their evening.

"Well, you've got a point, Doc." She gave a lusty sigh. Then, her emerald green eyes glimmering, she rose on tiptoe and fitted her lips to his. Her kiss was everything he wanted, sweet and evocative, playful and tempting.

Excitement building, body hardening, he threaded his hands through her hair and kissed her back. Not stopping until she trembled in response and tore her lips from his.

"I suppose it would be prudent to take advantage of our—" breathing raggedly, she began to unbutton his shirt "—solitude."

He pretended shock. "Why, Nurse Monroe! Are you coming on to me?" Sliding his hands down her hips, he moved to shift places with her, so her back was to the counter. His hands planted on either side of her, trapping her between the cabinets and his tall body.

Looking delighted to be his sensual captive, she wreathed her arms about his neck, bringing him closer still, and pressed her breasts against his chest. "Hmm, I think I am. Got a problem with that, Doc?"

He laughed huskily, loving this naughty side of her. "None at all." He eased his hands beneath her blouse and found her breasts, unclasped her bra. Her nipples were as taut with desire and silky warm as he recalled. He could tell by her shallow breathing how aroused she already was. Then he fused his mouth to hers, enjoying the way she opened her lips to the plundering exploration of his tongue. Responding with a hunger and need that matched his own.

"Bed," she whispered.

With the ache inside him growing, he kissed his way down her neck, to the open collar of her blouse, to the U of her collarbone.

"Eventually," he promised, knowing the longer they heightened the anticipation, the greater the payoff would be.

She arched against him, gasping when he opened

her blouse all the way and his lips reached her breasts, closing around the tips.

She purred as the pleasure seemed to ripple through her. Never one for passivity, she tugged the hem of his shirt from the waistband of his jeans. Swiftly, the buttons came undone. Her hands found him, too, and his muscles clenched as she touched the skin of his pecs, his tight nipples, the hair on his chest...

"Thought I was in charge here," he gasped. He undid the waistband of her slacks. Eased his hands beneath. Found her silky, warm, wet.

She kicked free of her clothes. Divested him of the rest of his. Surged up against him once again. "Equal opportunity lovemaking, didn't you know?"

He chuckled, pleased. "I do now."

Naked, they came together against the wall. She molded her body to his, kissing him again and again and again.

The ache inside him growing, he stepped between her legs. Taking both her hands in his, he lifted them over her head, pinning them there.

"Looking for a sweet spot?" she asked breathlessly.

He laughed and dropped his hands to trace the enticing womanly curve of her derriere. "Actually, quite a few..." Parting her thighs with his knee, he moved closer, found one, then another and another.

Clearly impatient for more, she groaned and rubbed her body against his, rising to meet him, the pinnacle of her release taking them by surprise.

"Now..." she whimpered, still shaking.

Glad to oblige, he moved inside her, taking the tremors to new, more powerful depths. The magical connection between them spiraled. And Jack knew the terms of their bargain...this Christmas...was just the beginning.

He lifted his head. Smiled down into her eyes.

"Once again, spectacular," she said.

His need to make her his intensified, not just for the season, but for all time. He stepped back and lifted her into his arms. "Then I'm assuming you won't mind if we do it again?" He carried her the short distance to her bed.

She chuckled softly. "You're indefatigable." She opened her arms to let him back in.

And with good reason. He was trying to achieve a Christmas miracle here.

"Let's just say," he murmured, joining her beneath the sheets and picking up right where they'd left off, "you inspire me."

Chapter Thirteen

"Be prepared for questions," Jack whispered in Bess's ear Wednesday evening as he took her coat. "The Terrific Trio is in full interrogation mode tonight."

Chuckling, Bess gazed up at him. "Am I going to need a lawyer?"

"Maybe."

"Thanks for the warning," she quipped. Then, sensing he was thinking of kissing her, she quickly moved to sidestep the sprig of mistletoe still hanging in his foyer.

Just in time, as it happened.

Lindsay, Chloe and Nicole raced through the hallway from the rear of the house and dashed toward her. All three had red monogrammed aprons on over their dresses, and Santa hats on their heads.

"Daddy said he doesn't want to wear his apron," Lindsay reported.

"But we said he should," Nicole chimed in.

"'Cause he'll get *messy*, if he doesn't," Chloe said.

Sensing a slight change of subject was in order, Bess asked, "Where's Mrs. D.?" She had been counting on Jack's nanny to help supervise the decorating.

Jack stood with one brawny shoulder braced against the breakfast room portal. In jeans, sneakers, and a long-sleeved cotton shirt that brought out the cobalt blue of his eyes, with his short hair neatly brushed and the barest hint of stubble on his face, he looked like any dad set to enjoy a relaxing evening at home with his family.

Except she wasn't his wife or his daughters' mommy... Nor, given his reluctance to ever remarry, was she ever likely to be.

Picking up on her sudden ambivalence, he flashed a reassuring smile. "They were unexpectedly one judge short at the ugly Christmas sweater competition over at Laramie Gardens senior living facility." He pushed away from the door and came to stand next to her. "Mrs. D. went to help out."

"That was nice of her. I hear it's pretty competitive."

"Yeah, it is. Comically so." He gave her an appreciative once-over, settled on her face. "Not to worry. Mrs. D. got us all set up this afternoon, by preassembling all four houses."

Bess blinked in surprise. "There are only four?"

Lindsay retorted, "Daddy says you can decorate his, Bess, 'cause he doesn't really like icing stuff all that much. But we think everybody should *share*. Because sharing is fair."

Bess smiled, the affection she felt for all three girls pouring through her. "It certainly is."

Nicole wrapped her arms around Bess's waist. "Do you like candy?"

Bess stroked Nicole's golden curls. "Yes, I do."

"Good, because we've got gumdrops and chocolate kisses and all sorts of colored ones. Fruity kind and chocolate kind and peppermint sticks, too."

Chloe joined the fray shyly. "Here's your apron, Bess." It was also red, though not monogrammed.

"Daddy?" Lindsay challenged.

Jack locked eyes with Bess, as if he knew what was coming, then made a face. The girls thrust another plain red apron at him. Bess soon saw what the problem was. It was too tiny for his large frame. He could barely get it around his neck. It only half covered his chest, and there was no way it was going to fasten.

Nevertheless, seeing how important it was to his girls that they all be similarly outfitted, Bess called on Jack's usual sportsmanship and suggested, "Maybe if you have an old necktie, I can fix you up."

While he was gone, she went ahead and put her apron on, as well as the Santa cap the girls gave her.

"Don't you look festive," Jack drawled upon his return.

She motioned for him to bend down. She slapped a hat on his head, purposefully doing it so it fell over one of his eyes. The girls erupted in giggles. "You look festive, too!"

Bess fastened his apron, with the necktie, and then they settled down to decorate, and after some convoluted discussion, they finally decided to do the three girls' houses first, with Jack and Bess assisting. The icing was premade, too, so all they had to do was smear the gingerbread rooftops.

A task easier said than done by his three young girls. The white icing was soon everywhere, in their hair, on their clothes and faces and hands. Somehow Jack and Bess got it all over themselves, too.

And of course there were more questions, as Jack had warned. Lots and lots of questions. "Do you like to make gingerbread houses, Bess?" Lindsay asked.

"Yes."

"Did you do one this year?" Nicole wanted to know.

"Not for quite a while."

Chloe paused. "Did you make cookies?"

"Um, not yet," Bess admitted reluctantly. She'd been too busy being pursued by Jack and pursuing him a little in return.

Lindsay licked icing off a spoon. "Then how are you going to leave them out for Santa?"

Jack cut in, "Santa doesn't come to Bess's house, remember?"

Nicole's eyes widened. "Then who does?" She turned to face Bess, and her arm hit the house she was decorating, pushing it precariously close to the table's edge.

Bess caught the confection before it could fall, and unobtrusively pushed it back to safety. "Usually I end up going over to one of my brothers' or sisters' houses on Christmas Day."

"But what about Christmas morning?"

"Well, before my twin sister, Bridgett, got married, we always had a sleepover on Christmas Eve."

Lindsay's eyes widened. "Did you stay up till midnight talking and goofing around?"

"Pretty much. But now I usually sleep in." *Feel sorry for myself. Wish I had a husband to love and a family of my own, too.*

"So you're all alone?" Nicole noted plaintively.

Ignoring Jack's quiet, intent gaze, Bess soothed all three girls with a smile. "For a little while—"

"Daddy, that's not fair," Lindsay interrupted before Bess could finish. "Bess shouldn't be all lonely on Christmas!"

"Yeah, Daddy," Chloe said fiercely.

Nicole added, "She should come and spend it with us!"

Jack had figured his girls would find a way to put him and Bess on the spot. They had been doing that a lot lately. Maybe because they sensed that his feelings for their old family friend, which had always been warm and cordial, had taken on a more intimate hue.

He turned to Bess, who was bright red, then said as casually as possible, "This wasn't how I was planning to broach the subject—" not anywhere close, actually "—but I agree with the girls." He looked deep into Bess's eyes, doing his best to let her know how much he had come to care for her. "It's not fair you are alone on Christmas Eve, and again on Christmas morning. It's not fair," he added before he could stop himself, "you don't have everything you always wanted."

Briefly, the girls looked confused.

Bess stiffened. "I know you're all feeling sorry for me right now, but it's not necessary. The truth is, I have a lot of invitations and I could go to a lot of other places if I wanted to do so. I just don't want to, well, horn in on someone's private—" she looked as if she was going to say *affair*, but decided instead to say "—present-unwrapping."

Nicole's brow furrowed. "What does that mean, Daddy? Bess doesn't want to ham in?"

"Horn in," Jack corrected. "And it means she is being as gracious as always. But when it comes to our family, I think we—" his gaze encompassed all three daughters meaningfully "—are all in agreement that we would really like to have you here with us this year, on Christmas Eve, when we go to my parents' open house at their ranch, as well as on Christmas morning." He gave her a significant look. "For a whole host of reasons."

"Yes, Bess! You should come!" the girls pleaded.

"Well," Bess said eventually. She watched Jack's daughters press pieces of candy into the still sticky icing. "Maybe I could drop by for a little while?"

Jack kicked back in his chair. "To both?"

Her head lifted and her green eyes locked on his. She nodded shyly. "If it's okay with your parents."

Exhaling slowly, he found himself wanting to be the man of her fantasies. She was certainly the woman of his.

"You've got to know it will be more than okay," he said softly. And to emphasize his point, he inclined his head in the direction of the mistletoe his mother had hung in the foyer at the other end of the hall.

Bess's eyes glittered with the memory of their last kiss there.

"But I would probably drive out separately on Christmas Eve, because…um…I've got stuff—" like two puppies to take care of, he remembered "—going on here in town."

"That would be fine," Jack said. "I'll text you the details about the open house, and we will see you there."

"As your platonic compadre," Bess confirmed.

He nodded his reluctant agreement. They would have to change that eventually. But right now, what they had discovered was so fragile and new, he didn't want to risk messing it up.

"Christmas morning will be a lot more private and relaxed," he promised.

The girls, understanding only that their wish had come true, jumped up and down.

"Yeah!"

"Hurray!"

"I'm so happy!"

They certainly would be, to have Bess sharing the Christmas holiday with them. Seeing his youngest was lagging behind her older sisters, Jack reached over to help put colored chocolate candy pieces on Chloe's gingerbread house. "Just make sure you get here before 5:00 a.m. so you don't miss all the excitement," he told Bess.

Her festive laugh filled the air. "I've heard it gets started early."

"You have no idea."

For the next few minutes, they all worked in companionable silence, adding gumdrops and peppermint candy canes, rainbow-colored candy pieces and chocolate kisses until there was literally no more room to add any more.

"Now, Daddy and Bess," Lindsay directed, "you do one together and we will watch!"

The girls got up and motioned Jack and Bess to sit together in front of the remaining undecorated gingerbread house. Bess focused on spreading the icing, while Jack decorated as fast as he could.

"Are you coming to our preschool sing-along tomorrow night with Daddy?" Nicole asked. The girls lingered nearby, eating candy.

Bess paused, as if not certain how to answer that.

Three little faces fell in heart-wrenching disappointment, the kind that came mostly at times like this, when other kids they knew had both a mommy and a daddy to share their joy.

"Don't you want to hear us sing?" Chloe's lower lip trembled.

"It's all Christmas songs!" Lindsay, who would be appearing as a preschool alumna, informed her.

Nicole nodded urgently. "We're going to be on the stage and everything! And then we get to go to Uncle Dan and Aunt Kelly's afterward, and have pizza and cookies and all sorts of stuff with the cousins!"

"Please, Bess?" Chloe begged. "Please say you'll come."

"It won't be as much fun if you don't," Lindsay said, near tears.

Looking a little misty herself, Bess hugged the girls close, in turn. "Of course I would love to be there," she said thickly. "So yes, I will meet you all at the preschool. And go to the party afterward, too."

Once again, Jack noted, she was nixing anything that would make it more like a date.

"Sorry about that," Jack said, after the girls were in bed and he came back downstairs. Bess had already carefully carried the four creations to the dining room table for display. Together, they went back to the kitchen to clean up the gingerbread house decorating disarray.

He brought the wastebasket over, and they both got down on the floor to pick up the pieces of candy scattered about the breakfast room floor, before it became an even bigger mess.

"The girls asked me earlier about the sing-along," he said. "I knew you were still on the fence, and I told them I wasn't sure you were going to be able to attend."

Bess picked up the last two stray candies. "Well, I am happy it all worked out and that I can come."

"Me, too. But you seem upset with me." He pushed

to his feet and offered her a hand up. "Want to tell me why?"

She let go of his hand as soon as she was standing and moved to put distance between them. "Actually, I'm upset with both of us," she confessed. "Our conversation with the girls made me realize that up until now, I've only been thinking about what the two of us are getting out of our holiday arrangement. I didn't give any thought to who else could be hurt by our recklessness, and I need to do that, Jack." She swallowed hard. "So do you."

Enjoying the way she looked in faded jeans, boots and a snug-fitting V-necked sweater, with her hair forming a soft cloud about her face, he managed to point out, "The girls don't know we're seeing each other."

She gathered up the stack of soiled aprons and carried them into the laundry room. The washer was empty, so she slid them in, along with a few holiday dish towels. As comfortable in his home as her own, she added detergent and switched it on. "But they know us both well enough to sense that something is different when we're together now. They may not be able to actually identify it per se, but they know the situation is changing."

He returned her troubled look, knowing she would give him everything she had—except a way past the barricades guarding her heart. "You want to know why the girls intuited the shift in our attitude."

Working like the team they usually were, he sprayed down the counters while she tore off lengths of paper towels. "It's not that you've agreed to spend time with us on Christmas this year," he told her as he cleaned. He watched her stretch across the island and do the same. "Or that you've gone to so many McCabe family social gatherings with us."

His gaze sifted over the stiffness of her slender shoulders as she scrubbed stuck-on-frosting with a vengeance.

"Because you've been accompanying us to the McCabe family potlucks a lot for the last couple of years, as a much-treasured platonic family friend." He threw his paper towel in the trash and moved toward her. "It was the fact that you hesitated to accept their invitation to watch them do something at school."

Guilt, and something else he couldn't quite identify, gleamed in her dark green eyes.

He cupped her shoulders between his palms and continued, "That resistance on your part was what hurt their feelings. The fact that, for the first time ever, you didn't jump at the chance to spend time with them."

And frankly, it had surprised him, too. Usually, when it came to his girls, and to him, there were no limits on what Bess would give.

He felt the same about her. When she needed him, he was there.

She was silent a long moment, her expression inscrutable. "I know that, Jack." She walked over to straighten the chairs around the table. Keeping her voice low, she confessed, "And that, in turn, makes me worry that they're starting to get a little too dependent on me, under the circumstances."

She drew a bolstering breath that lifted her breasts. "And that when the holiday is over and our temporary fling ends, they will somehow pick up on that, too, and be even more upset." Moisture glimmered in her eyes. "And I don't want to hurt them, Jack."

Neither did he. He closed the distance between them and took her in his arms, smoothing the hair away from her face. "So maybe we shouldn't try to go back to being just friends." He hoped she would see things his way.

He rubbed the pad of his thumb across the silky curve of her cheek. "Maybe we should try letting this evolve naturally and see where it will lead instead."

Bess flattened her hands across the hard wall of his chest, with enough force that he released her. "Right now I know this all seems like an awful lot of fun, and I won't deny it has been. But when the novelty and convenience of this arrangement fades, it will more than likely create a whole lot of new tension or awkwardness. Which, in the midst of the midwinter doldrums, might be even more apparent to the girls than what they've already picked up on."

The fact she was so sensitive to his girls' needs was great. But her willingness to sacrifice what they had? Not so much...

He wanted them to look for an alternative to simply ending this once the holidays were over. Especially now that they were seeing how much they were starting to mean to each other.

He frowned. "I'm not like the guys you were involved with in the past, Bess."

"I know that," she returned matter-of-factly. "But none of my exes meant for us to use each other, either. Yet, at the end of the day, that is exactly what we did."

Jack knew he had dropped the ball with Bess, backing her into a relationship with him the way he had. He also knew he still had time to turn things around and show her just how serious he was about not only continuing their affair, but finding a way to build a happy and fulfilled life together for all of them in the future.

Unfortunately, she left shortly after their talk on Wednesday evening, avoided him at the hospital on

Thursday and managed not to sit anywhere remotely close to him at the preschool sing-along.

He knew she needed her space, and he tried to give it to her after the event, by focusing on riding herd on all three of his girls while simultaneously saying a personal hello and merry Christmas to every parent he knew.

The ploy worked, until he arrived at Kelly and Dan's home. No sooner had he walked in than he spotted Bess handing off her contribution to the meal, a tray of cookies.

Nicole and Chloe made a beeline for her, engulfing her in a big hug. Lindsay stayed behind to loudly and excitedly point out the obvious. "Daddy! Bess! There's more mistletoe!"

Everyone turned. Amped up after their sing-along, Nicole and Chloe grabbed Bess's hands and dragged her in his direction. Lindsay did the same with him.

Nicole shouted, "Kiss!"

Chloe clapped her hands. "Right now!"

Bess came nearer to Jack and gave him a bright smile that clearly meant *this is exactly why I didn't want to come here tonight.*

All eyes were upon them. Seeing a way out, Jack grabbed Bess before she could ease away. The skin of her wrist felt silky soft and warm in his palm.

"Trust me on this," he whispered.

"Really?" she murmured back sweetly, looking like what she really wanted to do was kick him in the shin. "I don't think so."

Meanwhile, more McCabes and their loved ones gathered round.

"Go for it, bro," Chase encouraged.

Jack shrugged at the crowd. "You really want us to kiss?"

"Yes!" the girls chorused, jumping up and down.

"Kiss…kiss…kiss!" some of the little cousins chimed in.

"Well, all right, then!" Jack let go of Bess long enough to scoop up Nicole and Lindsay. He gave her a look. Bess got the idea and picked up Chloe. Then he put the girls between them and smacked each of their cheeks, in turn, while Bess did the same.

The girls erupted in giggles.

They set down the kids, and Jack delivered the perfunctory peck on the cheek he knew Bess would approve of.

Preventing a request for an encore, he rubbed his hands together. "Now, where are all those cookies I've been hearing about?" he asked.

"Cookies!" the kids yelled again and raced off to the dining room buffet.

"So you and Bess are dating now?" Rachel asked in obvious approval.

Jack knew Bess wouldn't want him to reveal anything about what was going on between them to anyone in his family, so he feigned surprise. "No, of course not, Mom."

Too late, he noticed Bess lingering nearby, and worse, she was definitely within earshot. Flushing, she promptly moved off to help with the chaos in the dining room. He moved to assist, too, but found himself lassoed by his mother and cornered in the foyer instead.

"How about helping me bring something in?" she asked.

"Happy to help," Jack said. Just not happy to answer more prying questions.

"So you're not dating," Rachel said as he escorted her out to the curb where his Dad's luxury pickup was parked. "Yet you've been together every single night for how long now?"

Not long enough by Jack's standards.

"Where'd you hear this?"

"Gossip grapevine."

"What's your point, Mom?"

Rachel opened up the rear passenger door. "I don't want to see Bess hurt."

Anger surged. "You really think I'd do that?"

Rachel pointed to a flat of kiddie juice boxes. "Not intentionally."

He picked them up. "But?"

Rachel brought out another flat, this one containing adult-size peppermint brownies from the local bakery. She set those on top of the juice boxes. "It can be easy to take someone for granted without actually meaning to, especially when you've spent as much time hanging out together as you and Bess have these past two years."

Resentment roiling through him, Jack watched his mother close the truck door. "Believe me, Mom, I know how much Bess has given of herself to me and the girls."

"Just make sure you honor that."

"No worries," he returned resolutely. "I intend to do just that."

The question was how, given the parameters he and Bess had already set up.

"Are you sure you're okay?" Bridgett walked Bess out of Kelly and Dan's house the back way, so they could avoid the crush of family.

Bess looked at her very pregnant twin. Mere days away from giving birth, she radiated a peaceful serenity Bess could only hope to one day achieve.

"Yes. I just have a little headache."

Bridgett took her elbow and steered her toward a seat on the wraparound porch. As they sank down on the cushioned wicker, they admired the twinkling Christmas lights decorating the pretty residential street. "Don't shut me out." She drew her sweater close. "C'mon. What is going on?"

Bess knew she had to confide in someone. "It's just been a week of a lot of ups and downs. And I just need a little space, you know?"

Bridgett nodded, still worried.

They rose. Hugged. "You know I'm always here for you, even if I am married now," Bridgett said quietly.

"I know." But it wasn't the same.

And maybe, Bess thought as she said goodbye to her sister and headed home, it wasn't supposed to be. As adults, shouldn't they all be spreading their wings, making their own families and lives? And although earlier in the season, Bess had sort of grouchily blamed fate and resented everyone else for their success and happiness compared to her own lonely existence, now she knew that it was all on her.

The problem was, she still didn't know if she was doing the right thing, getting so involved with Jack. Would she be as content as he was to simply let things unfold, in whatever way it was meant to?

The impulsive side of her said yes.

However, the more cautious part of her knew he could shatter her heart to pieces, if she weren't careful. And she *had* to be careful.

She went home and spent the rest of the evening doing chores. At ten thirty, she washed her face and brushed her teeth and changed into her coziest pair of red plaid flannel pajamas and slippers.

Of course, that was when her doorbell rang.

She didn't really need to look through the window to know who was there. Her heart accelerating, she opened the front door. Felt a mixture of emotions—joy, anxiety, frustration, need—pour through her.

Doing her best to appear much less overwrought than she actually felt, she took in his sober gaze and ruddy cheeks, which indicated, along with no SUV in the driveway, that he had walked over from his house. "A little late to be paying social calls, isn't it, Doc?"

"Bridgett told me you left with a headache. You weren't answering my texts. I wanted to make sure you were all right."

"As you can see—" she did a little pirouette "—I'm fine."

"I don't know. There was a lot of McCabe family energy tonight." He reached up to tuck an errant strand of hair behind her ear.

Bess tingled in delight.

"Sometimes we can be a lot to handle."

The memory of the wildly enthusiastic "kiss, kiss, kiss" chant from the kids brought new heat to her face. Telling herself it was the cold air coming in from outside that was tautening the tips of her breasts, Bess shrugged. "As can the Monroe clan. The bane of coming from a large family, I guess. So." She feigned cool indifference. "Thanks for checking up on me. And good night…" Still feeling peeved and out of sorts, she shut the door.

He rang the bell again.

She opened the door.

The corners of his sensual lips turned up. He seemed to know the effect his easy masculine presence always had on her, darn it. "Invite me in so we can really talk."

She swept a hand through her hair, or tried to, until she remembered she had put it up in a clip. Talking would lead to understanding, which would lead to forgiveness, which would lead to… "Actually, Doc, it's kind of late."

He gave her a long look that set her heart to racing all the more. The sadness and uncertainty she'd been feeling came and went in his expression. "Neither of us is going to sleep if we leave it like this," he said.

She recalled what he'd said about the long silences from Gayle, when they'd had a falling-out, and how he never wanted to repeat that. She knew it wasn't a good habit for her to get in, either. "Okay." She capitulated, as he had to have known she eventually would, and opened the door wide. Shutting it after him, she walked through the living area to the galley kitchen, where she looked for something else to do.

Jack spoke first. "I know you heard what my mom asked me about us."

Spying the green clean light on her dishwasher, she opened the door. The residual heat and steam of the last cycle rushed out, forcing her to step back and right into him.

She bumped up against his solid male warmth. Felt again the tingling rush of awareness.

He reached out to steady her. He went on, "I also know you heard what I said to her in return."

No, of course we're not dating… As if it would never ever be possible.

Tamping down her hurt, Bess regained her balance and moved away. Pretending the uneven meter of her breath was due to her near spill and not the hunger she noted in his intent cobalt blue gaze, she pulled out one rack, then the other to let them cool, then moved to stand opposite him.

"You were correct. We aren't dating."

Now it was his turn to look offended. "It feels like it."

"I know." Bess folded her arms. "And maybe that's the problem with this whole friends-with-benefits arrangement during this incredibly sentimental time of year. The lines are getting blurred."

"So, as I said to you the last time we talked about this, then maybe we should alter them. Do away with any set end date to our relationship."

Bess briefly closed her eyes and sighed, wishing this was all so different, that they were in love. "Oh, Jack. That's what made our affair palatable in the first place."

"For you, maybe." He removed the clip from her hair, ran his fingers through the mussed strands. He let his gaze rove over her face, as if memorizing every inch. Then murmured, "Not for me, Bess. Never for me."

Their lips met, and the world fell away.

All she knew was the comfort of his mouth moving over hers, and the mesmerizing power he seemed to hold over her heart. As he continued to kiss her, she couldn't recall ever feeling this turned on, and she knew she had never been with anyone who felt this right for her, this real, this solid.

That had to count for something. Didn't it?

"Tell me you want this," he whispered between slow, seductive kisses.

Bess trembled. "I do." She led him into the shadowy confines of her bedroom. "Heaven help me...help us both... I do."

Then his mouth was on hers again in a kiss that was shattering in its protectiveness and its possessiveness. He deepened the kiss, his palms on her back, drawing her intimately close. She felt his hardness, his heat, and wrapped in each other's arms, they tumbled onto her bed. As they settled onto the pillows, the affection in Jack's eyes was all the incentive she needed.

Maybe they didn't have all the answers now, Bess thought, as they undressed each other, slowly and reverently, but she had to have faith, as Jack already did, that the knowledge they required would come in time.

And in the meantime, there was no denying the yearning deep inside of her.

Afterward, they clung together. As they lay together, face to face, and worked to slow their breathing, Bess felt a sense of warmth and peace that touched her to the core. Was lifelong happiness around the corner for them both after all? She could only hope...

The next week flew by. Jack and Bess took the girls to San Antonio to ice-skate and see a holiday Christmas play for kids. Together, the five of them traversed the River Walk and viewed the dazzling holiday lights display. And for the first time in what seemed like forever, Jack had a sense of what it would be like to risk the cruel whims of fate and have a complete family again. Back in Laramie, he and Bess spent time together alone, too. Making sure to find time to cuddle every night, in and out of bed.

Neither of them talked about the future. Both focused solely on the minute they were in. An approach that worked to keep them happy and content.

But as the weekend neared, change in the form of two new puppies, about to come home, altered the horizon yet again. Bess was happy yet distracted when she came over for pizza on Friday night with the girls. She nixed the idea of seeing him alone later, as had become their private routine, because, she said, she had so much to do to get ready for the trip to Winfield Ranch the following day.

Her excuse made sense. Yet Jack thought it might be something else, like the fact she had realized they had just a week left on their deal to help each other through Christmas. As well as the need to continue to sort out her feelings.

He was okay with that. If she needed space to come to the conclusion he already had, that they were meant to be together for more than just a few heady weeks, he was willing to give it to her. Just as she had always given him space when he needed it in the past.

She looked better, more herself, when he picked her up on Saturday to go to Winfield Ranch to sign the adoption papers and collect their puppies.

Four hours later, when the two of them were seated on the floor of the gated-off portion of her living room and finally had the puppies situated, she looked even happier.

"Oh, Jack," she gushed, as Princess Abigayle and Lady Grace climbed up onto her lap and simultaneously licked her under her chin. "I think I'm in heaven!"

She certainly looked blissed out, with two adorable fluffy golden retrievers on her lap, paying homage to her in every way they could. Jack captured the moment with the camera on his cell phone and then promptly texted the pictures to her.

"You know what Betty said." He grinned as the lovefest continued. "When they kiss you on the face, it means they are accepting you as their mother."

Tears of joy spilled out of her eyes. "I remember." She laughed as one of the puppies caught her mouth with a big sloppy kiss. "Okay, my little pumpkins, let's settle down a bit."

They stopped long enough to gaze up at her ador-
ingly, their little tails wagging, then snuggled back down
in her arms.

Leaving their mama dog had been traumatic. The
pups had turned to Bess for comfort from the moment
they left, while Jack drove. And now that they were
home, they were still looking to her for comfort.

"This is like having twins," she said.

Except it was her sister Bridgett who was having the
human twins. And though he knew Bess both loved
and valued this kind of happiness, she also deserved
the satisfaction of having a husband and children who
loved her, too.

But right now, as she snuggled and doted on the adorable puppies, she didn't seem to be thinking about all
that was still lacking in her life. She released a contented sigh. "Maybe this is what's meant for me, Jack.
I mean, maybe it's my fate?"

"Maybe," Jack said. But maybe there was more in
store for her, too. Lots more. Happiness he could help
her achieve.

Oblivious to his thoughts, Bess continued stroking
the puppies' soft golden fur. She shook her head in won-
derment. "I never understood when people said that
having a new puppy was like having a new baby." She
laughed as the pups gazed up at her as if they understood every word she said. She rubbed them tenderly
behind their ears. "And now, at least for a bit, I've got
two!"

Aware he had never seen her look so radiant, Jack
asked, "You're sure it's not going to be too much?"

Bess shook her head as one of the puppies finally
climbed off her lap and ambled over to see him. Her
buddy soon followed. "This is why I saved up my va-

cation all year, so I'd be able to really enjoy this prime bonding time. I don't have to go back to work until after the New Year."

Soon Jack had a lapful of puppies, too. "I'm off between Christmas and New Year's, too. So maybe we can do a lot of this together then?"

Bess flashed a contented smile. "I'd be happy to arrange puppy playdates at both our houses, as well as share whatever hands-on wisdom I develop during the first week."

It was just too bad they couldn't all be under the same roof. Enjoying the experience together.

Not that Bess wasn't looking deliriously happy as it was. No, she was definitely all aglow.

But Jack knew he had the power to make her even happier. Of course, since they were just friends with benefits and she was reluctant to take it any further than that, at least for right now, her childlessness technically wasn't his problem.

And yet, Jack thought, still watching her intently, somehow it was.

Chapter Fourteen

Jack headed for the hospital, early the next morning. He had an hour before he had to prepare for his first surgery of the day, which gave him plenty of time to do the research.

Cup of coffee in hand, he settled down in front of his office computer. The information he wanted was easy to find. He was so engrossed in studying it, he didn't hear the knock on his door, or was even aware of someone coming in, until he caught a drift of familiar perfume.

Bess.

Looking like she had just tumbled out of bed and thrown on the first thing she could find before heading for the hospital.

Not about to let her see what was on his computer screen, he hit Escape and the data disappeared. He rocked back in his swivel chair. "What's going on?" he asked, noting she wasn't in uniform. So this couldn't be work-related. She was still on vacation. "Everything okay?"

She stuck her hands in her pockets and peered at him curiously. "I was going to ask the same of you," she said as if intuiting that something was up. "I saw your Suburban in the lot when I came in. Figured you'd be in emergency surgery, and yet here you are—" she cocked her head "—doing...?"

He told her what little he could. For now, anyway. "I'm checking statistics for surgical techniques."

She moved around his desk, perched on the corner and glanced over at his blank screen. "You know," she teased, "if I didn't know better, I'd think you'd just been doing something naughty."

He choked on his coffee, aware she didn't know how close to reality she was.

Dess clapped a hand over her lips. "I can't believe that just came out of my mouth." She leaned close enough to whisper, "See what being your lover has done to me?"

He rubbed his thumb along the inside of her wrist. "Hey, darlin', if that's where your mind is going, I can't say I mind a bit. As long as you and I are the starring players."

She uttered a low, sexy laugh. Looking heavenward, she said, "You are going to be the end of me, Doc."

He gripped her hand in his. "Seriously, if I looked guilty," he said quietly, "there's a reason."

She lifted her brow.

"I was fibbing when I implied what I was doing was work-related. Actually, it was personal. *Very* personal."

She inhaled. "Okay." Waited.

He turned her palm over and traced the lifelines with the pad of his thumb. Felt her soft skin heat in response. "I didn't want you to see what I was rescarching, because the subject matter had to do with your Christmas present."

She looked surprised. "We're doing that this year?"

Seeing a chink in her emotional armor, he nodded. "I'd like to. As long as it's okay with you."

She disengaged their palms and moved away, her guard up once again. "Listen, Jack. Just because I'm giving the girls something again this year and they always make something for me doesn't mean that you and I have to exchange gifts, too."

Refusing to let this be a roadblock, he rose and moved closer. "I want to do this, Bess," he said resolutely. "I didn't realize how much until this weekend."

Glowing with happiness, Bess cupped his biceps and gazed up at him. "Princess Abigayle and Lady Grace put you in the spirit, hmm?"

And you. Definitely you. "So what would you like?"

She dropped her hold on him. "You want me to just tell you?"

Jack sat on the edge of his desk. "Well, that's usually the way it works. Or at least it did with Gayle." He shrugged. "She'd give me specific ideas, and as long as I chose from that list, we'd be good as gold."

"Well, I hate to break it to you," she countered, looking a little hurt, "but that's not the way it works with *me*. You don't have to give me a gift... The time we have spent together has made me happy enough already. But if you do want to go down that path, then I'd rather you give me whatever you want me to have."

"So I'm on my own, then?" he asked. When it came to her, he was always up to the challenge.

Bess grinned. "Afraid so, Doc. Whatever it is has got to be a surprise. And not to worry." She patted him with a reassuring hand. "I'm sure I will love it."

Funny, Jack knew she would, too. He felt that in sync with her.

"So what are you doing at the hospital so early?" he asked curiously. Still dressed in a pajama top and jeans, no less. Her hair a sexy, tousled mess.

Bess collapsed into his desk chair. "Bridgett. She called from the ER a couple of hours ago, sure she was in labor. Turned out to be Braxton Hicks contractions."

"How did she take it?" Most new moms were distraught, hearing that diagnosis.

Bess made a sympathetic face. "Exactly like you'd think. She was upset and embarrassed. Felt that, because she's a nurse, she should have known the difference."

"But it was her first pregnancy." Robby was adopted.

"I know. That's what I told her." She rose gracefully. "Anyway, she went home half an hour ago. But they did tell her it could be any time now, since she is slightly dilated."

Jack reached out and kissed the back of her hand. "You seem really happy about this."

Bess leaned into his touch. "I am. I feel so close to her." Her voice caught. She shook her head in contentment. "It's like old times. The twin thing, of her joy being my joy. And it's at least partially due to you, Doc."

"What do you mean?" he rasped.

Her eyes sparkled. "You've given me hope again."

"Same here," he said gruffly.

Jack bent to brush his lips against hers.

When the tender caress ended, she studied him intently. "So what do you want for Christmas?"

Jack pretended to be affronted. "Hey, lady, you're on your own there."

She laughed as he meant her to, and he pulled her

close once again, giving her another sweet and tender kiss. "Seriously, whatever you give me, I'm sure I'll love it, too."

His decision finally made, Jack signed the receipt. The Laramie jewelry store, an institution in Laramie County, was the place where everyone he knew bought their engagement and wedding rings.

Wanting to ensure privacy, he'd made an after-hours appointment for 8:00 p.m., after his girls were in bed. Which had turned out to be a good thing. It had taken a lot of thought, to make his decision. The private showing area in back was elegant and quiet, the atmosphere relaxed, even though they'd stayed open just for him. Hence, he'd felt no pressure from the jeweler, just himself.

The store owner smiled. "The special lady in your life is going to love it."

Jack hoped so. He hadn't been this on edge since the last time he'd tried—and failed—to pick out an adequate surprise push gift for the woman in his life. Gayle hadn't liked it. And they'd ended up returning it. Or had planned to, until…fate had intervened.

Now that gift sat in a safety-deposit box at the bank, along with the other jewelry owned by his late wife, waiting for the day when his daughters would be old enough to inherit it.

"Especially when she understands the symbolism behind it," he continued.

"I hope so." Jack smiled.

The gift he'd chosen wasn't as straightforward as a ring. But it was still better than the diamond tennis bracelet or earrings that had been suggested.

"Would you like me to gift wrap it for you?"

Jack knew that wasn't his forte, either. "I'd appreciate it."

When he got home, he put the package in his sock drawer. Looked in on the girls. All were sound asleep. Mrs. D. was in the kitchen, doing some holiday baking. He chatted with her briefly, then ducked into his study and spent the rest of the evening doing more research on a subject he thought he would never need.

To his satisfaction, the prospects for an immediate solution were positive. He could only hope Bess would be encouraged by it, too.

The next morning, the holiday spirit in his home escalated. "Daddy, we want to talk to you about something," Nicole said.

"We want to get Bess a gift," Chloe added.

"You already made beautiful pictures for her. Remember?"

Lindsay frowned. "Besides that."

"We want to go shopping and *buy* something for her, too," Chloe said seriously. "And for her new puppy."

"And for us," Lindsay added.

This was definitely going somewhere. His little girls were in full group-planning mode. Jack sipped his coffee. "Did you all have something specific in mind?"

Vigorous nodding. "We want matching dresses. For Christmas. Like we used to wear with Mommy," Lindsay explained.

They had seen the pictures, even though they couldn't likely recall that.

"We all want to wear the same thing as Bess and we want her new puppy to wear the same dress, too."

Jack was momentarily dumbfounded. Although it was an incredibly cute idea.

"When is she getting her new puppy, Daddy?"

Jack answered carefully, lest he inadvertently give away any part of the surprise. "I think you'll be able to see Lady Grace on Christmas Day."

Nicole brightened. "Same time as our new puppy!"

"If Santa brings it," Chloe worried.

"I think he will," Lindsay declared.

The girls took a moment to think. "Well, then if he does, can we all wear matching dresses, including the two puppies?" Nicole asked.

"Well…" Jack's throat was suddenly a little rusty, at the thought his little girls might be every bit as ready for a new mommy as he was a new woman in his life. "First of all, I don't think dogs wear dresses." Although just trying to get them on the puppies would be riotous, a picture-worthy event he was sure.

"Oh, yes, they can!" Lindsay argued. "I've seen them, Daddy! At Halloween!"

That was true. More than one person had put their pet in costume during trick or treating.

"Puppies are different, though," Jack explained gently. "They're just little baby dogs, and they need to be comfortable. They don't like to wear things that scratch or itch or get in the way of whatever it is they are trying to do. Like run and jump and play. But," he continued when the trio of faces fell in disappointment, "they do wear collars and have leashes that are made of different colors, and I happen to know that Lady Grace is going to have a rose-colored collar. So you all could get a matching scarf and hat and gloves for Bess to wear when she walks her puppy on a leash outside. That would be a nice surprise." He thought. Hoped, anyway.

"But what about us, Daddy?" Nicole asked plaintively.

"I think you might want to get something to wear that is the same as the collar for the new puppy we hope Santa is going to bring us," Jack said. "Maybe something pink. And let Bess wear something that matches her new puppy. That way, we'll know who belongs with whom."

The girls fell silent, trying to wrap their minds around that. "And I am sure," Jack finished, "that you all will look very cute in whatever you wear."

"You know you don't have to keep bringing me lunch every day," Bess teased, when she met Jack at her door at noon on Friday. Although she did love seeing him come in, hair wind tossed, cheeks ruddy with the cold. And always so happy to see her and spend time with her, either during their casual midday encounters or leisurely late-evening lovemaking sessions.

She reached up to buss his cheek. "I can cook for myself, you know. Even with two puppies to watch over."

Jack leaned down to kiss her fully on the mouth. "I could just be here to see Lady Grace and Princess Abigayle," he teased, when the evocative caress ended.

Still tingling, she took the take-out bags. "I don't doubt for a minute the puppies are part of the allure. They've got me completely besotted, too."

Jack paused to study the sleeping puppies, who were curled up in their crates. "Adorable," he murmured.

Together they headed toward her dining room table. Missing work almost as much as she missed him when she wasn't with him, Bess laid out the silverware and napkins. He set out the chicken Caesar salads and iced teas, then held out her chair for her and waited until she slipped into it.

"So how are things at the hospital?" she asked.

With a smile, he sat down opposite her. "Unusually quiet, at least on the surgical wards. Everyone who can put off an elective procedure until after the holidays usually does. So right now we're just dealing with the emergent cases, which…knock on wood…have been few and far between for a change."

"And the girls?" Their knees touched briefly beneath the table. "Isn't today their last school day before the break?"

"It is." He laughed. "A fact that is only amping up their excitement."

"I can imagine." The only bad thing about having so much puppy duty was that she hadn't seen as much of his girls as she would have liked this week. But that would change soon, she knew.

"Naturally, we'd all like you to come over for pizza tonight," Jack continued, forking up a bite of salad.

"I could come for a little while." Bess stirred in the dressing with her fork. "But then I'll be right back on puppy detail." Her cell phone buzzed, signaling an incoming message. She reached around to get it from the pocket of her jeans, then, seeing the text pop up on-screen, flushed and promptly put it out of sight.

"Tim Briscoe again?" Jack asked lightly.

Telling herself he could not possibly be jealous of the pediatrician, not when she and Jack had been making love with as much passion and frequency as they had, she wrinkled her nose at him. "No." Holding her phone beneath the tabletop so he could not see, she typed a reply into her phone.

"Sure about that?"

So he was staking out his territory. She tried and failed not to be too thrilled. "Positive." Seeing he needed a little more information, she added, "Now that word's out Tim is looking for a girlfriend, women are coming to him and asking him out. So, I'm no longer needed as his matchmaker slash coach."

"Uh-huh." Jack sat back.

Another message dinged. She read the screen and typed something else.

"Then why all the secrecy?" he persisted, the desire she felt for him reflected in his eyes.

Already aching for another kiss, Bess turned off her phone and put it facedown on the table. "Oh, for heaven's sake! If you must know, my older sister Erin is helping me out with a portion of your present."

Now she had the good doctor's attention.

"It's something I would have a hard time getting done here, at least in a short amount of time, but is not an issue in Amarillo, where she and Mac and their kids live now. She's just been letting me know it's all taken care of and she'll be bringing the gift with them, to the Monroe Christmas party out at the family ranch tomorrow. So. Satisfied?"

Apparently so, judging by the smug male satisfaction in his gaze.

He tilted his head. Intrigued. "Is she making me a new pair of boots?" Erin was one of the premier custom bootmakers in the Southwest.

"Nice sleuthing," Bess said dryly. "And no, that's not it. She would have needed to have your measurements to do that." She lifted a staying hand. "And don't ask me anything else, because I'm not going to tell you anything more. You'll have to wait until Christmas to find out."

He chuckled. "So am I going to this party with you?"

It was a valid question, one she had been wrestling with for days. Seeing they had both finished eating, she rose and carried their take-out containers to the kitchen. "My sisters really want me to bring you and your girls."

He followed with the silverware and drinks. "Your brothers don't agree?"

Bess separated trash from recycling. "Gavin and Nick haven't said anything since the intervention."

"You're worried about what they'll think if you do bring me?"

"No." It was her life. She was going to live it in any way she saw fit.

"So what's the problem, then?"

She hesitated, not sure how much to reveal. "I've gone to a lot of McCabe gatherings, but—" she swallowed nervously "—you and the girls have never been to one of ours."

"About time, don't you think?"

"You'd really want to go?" she asked cautiously, wishing she knew what was in his heart. "Especially after what happened at the last McCabe get-together?"

His brows knit together, confirming her opinion this was dangerous territory. "You think we're going to face questions?"

Heck yes. "I think," Bess pushed on, figuring they might as well be completely candid about this, "when they all see us together and read our body language, that assumptions will be made."

"Assumptions are okay with me," he said gruffly.

But were they okay with her? Bess couldn't say. "Don't you have to get back to the hospital?"

"I've got the rest of the afternoon off."

So, in other words, she thought, they had plenty of time to settle this. It was a risk, bringing him into her life to that degree. "It will change things," she said quietly. In ways they might not even be able to predict.

Jack drew her close. "Haven't you heard?" He lowered his mouth to hers and delivered a searing kiss. "Change can be good."

"Well, in that case," Bess murmured, taking him by the hand and leading him down the hall to her bedroom. With a sweeping gesture, she invited him to sit on her bed. Then she began a slow and seductive striptease.

When she was clad only in her bra and panties, they changed places.

"My turn." Grinning, he took off his shirt and tie. Stripped off his shoes and pants. Clad only in his boxer briefs, he drew her to her feet. "Time to unwrap my present." He drew her bra straps down over her arms, exposing her erect nipples, before dropping it, along with her bikini panties, to the floor.

"And mine," she whispered playfully. Her hands whisked off his briefs, then closed over his pulsing hardness.

He guided her back down to the bed, stretched out facing her. Found her damp, silky, waiting. Then he positioned himself between her thighs, his lips lowering, suckling gently. She came up off the bed, her thighs falling even farther apart as he explored, touched, adored. Until she shattered in his arms.

Then it was her turn once again to worship him, and only when he could stand it no longer did she relent. Moving up to kiss him again, she clenched around him as he possessed her, making her his. She claimed him in return.

Until there was no more denying how much she wanted and needed him in her life. Until it wasn't just the holidays that were theirs for the taking, but the future, too.

It wasn't easy, given their penchant for spilling secrets, but during their pizza dinner Friday evening, Jack somehow managed to keep the girls from telling Bess what else they planned to give her for Christmas. He worried Saturday might be a lot harder, though, given the fact they had gone shopping for and wrapped said items that very morning.

"I don't understand why we can't give Bess her presents now." Nicole pouted as Bess parked her car in front of his house, got out and came up the walk, carrying food for the get-together.

Jack shepherded his girls outside to his Suburban. "Because we're going to wait until Christmas," he said. "And remember, it's a surprise."

Lindsay scowled. Chloe put her thumb in her mouth.

"Everything okay?" Bess asked cheerfully.

"Great," he said. And it was, since Bess had included him and his girls in this part of her life, for the first time.

"I promise you, we're going to have a lot of fun at my family's ranch," Bess told the kids, once they were all settled and on their way. "The Triple Canyon is not too far from your grandparents' ranch. It's very pretty out there. And it's going to be all decorated for Christmas. Plus, there are going to be lots of little boy and girl cousins for you to play with."

"Are they going to be dressed alike?" Nicole asked.

Jack tensed.

"What do you mean?" Bess turned to look at his daughters in the back seat.

"Are they going to be wearing the same as their mommies?" Lindsay elaborated.

Nicole scowled. "Daddy won't let us. He said it's not a good idea."

Oh, hell, there was no way this was going to turn out

well. "Girls…" Jack warned, giving them a censuring look in his rearview mirror. *Let's not bother Bess with our difference of opinion.*

Bess turned forward, still a little perplexed but ready to let it drop.

His daughters were not. Lindsay continued airing their grievance. "We wanted you to dress the same as all of us. So we would be matching. Like we did with our mommy. But Daddy said no."

That did it. Finally understanding, Bess turned a blotchy pink and white.

"It's not what you think," Jack whispered, able to see this adventure was quickly turning into a complete disaster.

Bess nodded, clearly doing her best to tamp down her hurt. "I think you should always do what your daddy says," she told his girls. "Now." She clapped her hands together with enthusiasm, declaring the whole matter closed for discussion. "Who wants to have another Christmas sing-along?"

Joyous shouts followed, and a whole host of carols occupied them during the rest of the journey. When they reached the ranch, Jack came around to Bess's side of the vehicle. "I can explain," he said swiftly, before he moved to let the girls out.

She'd had plenty of time to compose herself, and put up the emotional barriers he had so painstakingly taken down. "I know it's not what it sounded like," she said with a brisk smile.

Did she? It seemed as if she had a different take on the situation than what had transpired.

He had no chance to correct her, though, because

her siblings were already streaming out of the house to greet them.

Inside, the ranch house was full. There was her oldest sister, Erin, with her husband, Mac, and four children; Bess's youngest brother, Nick, and his wife, Sage, and their two young boys; her oldest brother, Gavin, his wife, Violet, and their two little girls; and of course, her very pregnant twin, Bridgett, with her husband, Cullen, and their son, Robby.

Before greetings were even finished, his daughters had their coats off and had forged right in to play with the younger set. Jack knew everyone there, so introductions weren't necessary.

As he spoke to everyone in turn, Bess left his side and went over to greet Bridgett. Jack wasn't sure if everyone else could tell, but he knew darn well there was a new aloofness between them. One that became ever more insurmountable with every second that passed.

He was still trying to figure out how and when he could get her alone, just for a minute, when she went over to sit beside her twin. They hugged. "You look exhausted," Bess said.

She received a deadpan look in return. "Thanks, sis."

"Seriously." Bess patted her twin's hand. "How are you doing? Your face is kind of red."

Bridgett winced in chagrin. "You mean from my Braxton Hicks debacle?"

"C'mon. Happens to every first-time pregnant mom!"

Bridgett eased a hand to her lower back. Rubbed. "Not NICU nurse moms. Or it shouldn't."

"I keep telling her to let it go." Erin settled in on the other side of Bridgett, like the mother hen she'd become to her orphaned sibs. "And try to sleep while she still can."

"Fat chance of that," Bridgett grumbled, completely hormonal. "They're wrestling in there, nonstop!" As if to demonstrate, her tummy punched visibly outward. "See what I mean?" She spread her hands wide, as everyone laughed.

Bess leaned down to put her ear to Bridgett's tummy. "Hey, there, little fellas. It's your aunt Bess speaking! Give your mommy a break, okay?" she said, as all the adults laughed again. "Mommy needs her sleep."

The room grew quiet. Bridgett looked down at her tummy. "I think it might have worked," she said in awe. "They're totally calm for the first time in days."

"What can I say?" Bess blew dust off her knuckles. "I've got the magic touch!"

"Which is great—" Bridgett grimaced, as if in pain "—except now I think I have to get up." She levered herself up off the sofa. "And go to... Oh, no. No, no!" she cried.

"What?" everyone asked in unison.

Bridgett clapped a hand over her tummy and looked at the liquid streaming down her legs, pooling at her feet. "It would appear," she said, deadpan, "that my water just broke."

The normally unflappable Cullen leaped up. "I'll get the truck!"

"I'll take care of Robby and Riot," Erin promised Bridgett.

Bridgett grabbed Bess's hand, in full twin mode once again.

"Not to worry. I'm coming with you," Bess soothed. She glanced at Jack, clearly thinking of him, the girls and the puppies.

"I've got it." Not caring who was watching, he went over to buss her temple and hug her close, then whispered, "Just go."

He would catch up with her later.

They would work out their problem when the time was right.

Chapter Fifteen

Jack walked into the hospital shortly after midnight, eager to see Bess. He knew he still had to explain the girls' comments to her, why he had felt it was presumptuous for the women in his life to all dress alike for this particular holiday.

But it wouldn't be, in the very near future.

That was, if all went as he wished. And Bess agreed with his plans for them. In the meantime, he hoped that the Christmas gift he had in his pocket would show her how he felt about her and their future in a way that words alone could not.

His heart racing, he stopped at the desk in the maternity ward, aware he hadn't felt such a complex mixture of emotions since the night his youngest child was born.

Elation and joy, over all he'd been given.

Worry and uncertainty, about how all the change

ahead and the advent of a new person would affect the delicate balance of his home life.

Confidence, that love and patience would help them find the way to the happiness they all wanted. And needed...

Because they did need each other, more than he had ever imagined they could.

"Looking for the Monroe twins?" the nurse behind the desk asked, oblivious to the hopeful nature of his thoughts.

"You got it."

She inclined her head to the other end of the hall. "They're all in room 221."

"Thanks." Jack strode toward his destiny.

The door was open. Bess was seated on the edge of the bed, next to her twin sister, a newborn nestled in her arms. She was gazing down at the infant with such incredible maternal tenderness Jack caught his breath.

She turned to him, tears of happiness glistening in her pretty green eyes. "Come see our new nephews," she whispered. "This is Colt."

"I've got Cade," Bridgett said.

Bess looked up at him, glowing with joy. "Aren't they gorgeous?" she whispered.

Gorgeous didn't begin to cover it, Jack thought, taking in their dark hair, angelic faces and sturdy little bodies. For the babies. Or the incredible woman in his life.

A woman he did not want to let go. Not ever. No matter the yuletide bargain they had made.

He nodded his agreement, suddenly feeling almost too choked up to speak. "They're perfect," he managed.

Cullen, who'd been filming on his phone, moved to include Jack in the shot, then shut it off and put it back in his pocket. He was grinning wildly.

"Congratulations," Jack told them both. Bridgett was occupied, so he contented himself with shaking his older brother's hand and embracing him in a hug.

Reluctantly, Bess stood and handed the infant back to his daddy. "Thanks for letting me be a part of this," she said.

"Thanks for being here," Cullen told Bess.

Bridgett chuckled. "You kept us both calm!"

"My pleasure." Bess put on her coat and picked up her bag. Bent to embrace her sister one last time, then Cullen. "Call me if you need anything," she told them.

Bridgett and Cullen nodded. "Will do," they promised, just as happily.

Jack and Bess eased from the room, her pique with him earlier seemingly mostly forgotten. Mindful of those who might be sleeping, they were quiet as they walked through the hospital, not speaking again until they were outside.

"How are the puppies?" Bess finally asked.

"Good. Mrs. D. came back in to help out tonight. So I was able to go back to your place and let the puppies out at six, feed them and make sure they did what they needed to do. I returned home for bedtime with the girls."

He steered her into the physicians' parking lot.

"Then I went back to your place around nine o'clock and hung out with the puppies for several more hours, getting them good and tired, before I came by to see if you needed a ride home." He wrapped an arm around her shoulders.

"I do." Briefly, she leaned into his touch, then turned her face up to his, her cheek brushing his shoulder in the process. "So if you wouldn't mind..."

"Have you had anything to eat?"

She wrinkled her nose. "A granola bar from the vending machine."

"Not to worry. Erin sent food home for you. It's in your fridge."

"That's my big sister. Always thinking ahead."

Jack held the door for her. She stepped in and let her head fall back against the seat.

He circled around and climbed behind the wheel. Tenderness swept through him. She'd watched over him and the girls so many times. Now it was his turn. He leaned over to stroke her cheek. "Exhausted?"

She nodded.

He drove the short distance to her house and, once again, got out and walked around to hold the door for her. He put a steadying arm about her waist as they moved up the walk and mounted the porch steps. When they walked in, the puppies barely lifted their heads, then sighed and settled back into sleep.

Bess grinned at him with appreciation. "You weren't kidding, Doc," she remarked. "You did get them tired."

He eased the bag off her shoulder, helped her out of her coat. "You know us Texans," he drawled, shedding his own jacket. "We aim to please."

"That we do." Bess unlaced the cranberry scarf from around her neck and turned to face him. The next thing he knew, she was in his arms. Their lips met halfway in an explosion of heat and need, want and passion. He gave her everything she asked for. Taking command. Losing himself in the touch and taste and feel of her. And still she kissed him, letting herself go in a way she never had before.

Yearning welled up inside him. He pressed the hardness of his body against the softer length of hers. Lost in the ragged intake of her breath and her low, shuddering moan.

* * *

In turn, Bess melted against Jack in boneless pleasure, savoring the feeling of his hard, warm chest against her breasts, the safety of being cradled in his strong arms. Lower still, his arousal pressed against her, weakening her knees.

For too long, she had tried to corral her feelings. Dismiss her physical needs. No more. She needed this closeness. Needed Jack. For who knew what the next days and weeks would bring?

He slid his hands down her arms, his palms tracing an erotic path, his lips pressing delicious kisses to her throat. "I want to take you to bed," he growled.

Trembling all the more, she flashed a crooked grin. "Don't let me stop you, Doc."

He chuckled softly. The next thing she knew, he'd tucked an arm beneath her knees and was carrying her through the kitchen, down the hall, to her bedroom. Her heart raced as he set her down and began to undress her. Admiring everything he revealed. And then his lips were on her flesh, sending her into a frenzy of want and need.

"Oh, Jack," she whispered, as a wave of pleasure detonated inside her.

"I know, darlin'," he murmured. "I'm feeling it, too." He held her until the aftershocks had passed, then lowered her onto the bed.

She watched him undress, taking his time about it, while she looked her fill.

"Seems like I'm not the only one aroused here," she murmured, as he stretched out beside her on the bed.

He grinned, all warm, satin skin and taut, hard muscle. "You like what you see, hmm?"

She kissed his shoulder, the center of his chest. "Very much."

The depth of his desire for her gave her the confidence to go after what she wanted, and before long, she had him on his back. She pleasured him as he had pleasured her, with hands and lips and tongue, not stopping until his body was throbbing as much as hers.

Then they changed places once again. He parted her thighs and took possession of her in the most intimate of ways. Her heart filling with sheer and utter bliss, she wrapped her arms and legs around him, arching against him, as he surged into her wet, slick heat. She moaned as he entered and withdrew in slow, shallow strokes. Then her pleasure intensified as he slid his hands beneath her hips, lifting her, driving deep.

Together, they soared toward a completion more stunning and fulfilling than anything she had ever dreamed. More incredible for her than the feel of him inside her was the knowledge that none of this—not their lovemaking or their time together—had to end. If they could find a way forward that would honor everything they had found, yet not ask either of them for what they could not quite give...

Afterward, he held her close and stroked her hair. "A pretty incredible evening, wasn't it?"

She lifted her head to gaze into his eyes. "Yes," she said softly. *And not just for everyone else, this time.* She drew a breath, admitting, "I'm so happy for Bridgett and Cullen."

"Me, too," he rasped. They snuggled some more, each of them lost in their own thoughts. Then he kissed the top of her head. Stroking a hand down her back, he said, "It's not just your twin, though. You really want to have a baby, too, don't you?"

The million-dollar question. Carefully, she admitted, "Yes, I do, but I also know it may not ever be in the cards for me." For the first time in her life, she was prepared to accept that if it meant she could have everything else she wanted. Like family and enduring love.

"What if," Jack ventured, rolling onto his side, so they had no choice but to look each other right in the eye, "I could give that to you?"

Bess's stunned reaction was not exactly what Jack had hoped to see. She struggled to sit up, covering her breasts with the sheet. "What are you talking about?"

Jack figured that was obvious. Still, he spelled it out for her wryly. "Specifically? Me, impregnating you."

Color flooded her high, sculpted cheeks. She narrowed her eyes at him. "Ah, need I remind you, Doc? You had a vasectomy."

"True. But I can also have surgery to have it reversed," he explained matter-of-factly. She shifted even farther away from him, and he sat up against the headboard, too. "Granted, my fertility will be reduced. There will only be somewhere between a 40 to 90 percent probability I can get you pregnant the old-fashioned way. But there are other options, too, if our initial attempts don't succeed."

She rose and slipped on a robe. "Why are you offering this?" she inquired, her face pinched with tension. "Just a month ago you said you were certain you didn't want to have any more children."

There were so many reasons Jack hardly knew where to start. He stood and pulled on his boxer briefs, pants, then his sweater. "You've done so much to help me and the girls the last three years. I want you to have everything you've ever wanted. To be as happy as you've made us."

Her eyes wide with disbelief, she walked into the kitchen and pulled two bottles of water out of the fridge. "But a baby, Jack…" she murmured in shock.

Okay, so maybe he had broached this badly. Their fingers brushed as she gave him a drink. He unscrewed the top of his bottle and drank deep.

"We have enough love to raise one," he pointed out, eyeing her over the rim of the bottle. He grinned as the possibilities took root. "Or even two, if you want."

She inhaled deeply, the action lifting the soft swell of her breasts. "We have to think about your girls, how they would react to something like this."

He tore his eyes from the shadowy V of her robe, wondering what it would take to get her to trust him on this. "They've already said they want to have a baby brother or sister, and they want you to have a baby, too. Plus, just as important, they need and want a mom. You've said you love Lindsay, Chloe and Nicole. And they all love and care about you as much as I do, Bess."

She studied him, her expression as closed as it was inscrutable. "Like family."

"Exactly," Jack confirmed, relieved she was beginning to get it. Still, she seemed offended, rather than as excited and happy as he felt deep inside.

Bess bit her lower lip. "A friendship-based arrangement like this would be no problem in places like Dallas or Houston, where the unconventional is more the norm. But in Laramie?" She drew a deep breath and seemed to choose her words with care. "As much as I'd like to do what would please me, I have to be realistic, too. And if we did something like this, without first getting married, people would *talk*, Jack. And that would hurt the girls. Plus any child or children we might have."

Glad she was warming to the idea so quickly, even if she was mostly considering the potential pitfalls of the situation, he countered, "Which is why we would need to get married as soon as possible if we want to go down this path. And I do, Bess."

"So people wouldn't talk?"

Jack nodded, excited by the prospect of finally moving past the friends-and-lovers-only phase of their relationship. "And," he said huskily, putting their water bottles aside before taking her hands in his, "because having us all together under one roof is the right thing to do."

She gazed up at him, her face growing pale. She turned and, clearly mindful of waking the puppies, quietly went back into the bedroom.

He followed and lounged in the doorway, his shoulder braced against the frame, giving her the space she seemed to require. "Look, I know this isn't the traditional route." They were talking babies before even getting engaged.

She backed into the comfy chair in the reading nook and sat down, as if her legs would no longer support her. "No kidding."

"But it would get you everything you want in life, in the fastest way possible. And to that end—" he removed the small jewelry box he'd put in his pants pocket before going to the hospital "—I got you this gift—"

She held her palm out, as if to keep him at bay. "No."

He stood there like the worst kind of fool, wondering how he could have misread the situation so badly. This should have been a joyous night. A harbinger of the Christmas to come. "No?" he repeated in surprise.

Lips compressed, she thrust her hands in the pockets of her robe. Meeting his gaze head-on, she said, "You're not thinking straight, Jack."

The hell he wasn't, he thought, staring back at her in escalating frustration. Maybe if she'd allow him to give her the gift he'd gotten her, she would see this was no spur-of-the-moment proposal.

But since she wouldn't, he would have to simply tell her what was in his heart. He would worry later about giving her the jewelry that he'd hoped would cement their relationship.

He moved several steps closer, hands spread imploringly. "I know it seems sudden. It's not. I want us to build a life and a family together, Bess."

She nodded her understanding but did not budge. Swallowing hard, she continued, "And that would be fine, if we loved each other, Jack. If we had the kind of close, familial relationship where it would be okay with you if the girls and I dressed alike, the way they used to with Gayle."

"Hey, now," he interrupted, not about to let that misconception stand, "my refusing to let them do that with you had more to do with the fact that we were rushing things, without laying the proper groundwork—like getting married and making it all official—than me objecting to you stepping in as their new mother. And I would have explained that to you at the time, if the girls hadn't been listening."

She stared at him as if finding his reasoning a little too convenient to be believed. She paused. "You're right," she said quietly, not bothering to mask her growing hurt. "We don't have that kind of relationship now. And we never will. Because we're just friends with temporary benefits."

She was acting like he had just permanently relegated her to the kind of second-best status she'd enjoyed with her previous boyfriends, instead of giving her the best gift that he could.

Heart clenching, he studied her stony expression. "And because you and I are just friends with temporary benefits, nothing else is ever going to be possible," he surmised grimly, beginning to see where this was going.

With a sad shake of her head, she confirmed, "Nothing like the lifelong love all our siblings have with their spouses. And that's what we both want and deserve, Jack. Not some half measure that will only lead to the kind of unhappiness I had at the beginning of the holiday season." Tears glittered in her eyes. "And I admit, in the sheer excitement of the holidays, I've been guilty of completely over-romanticizing everything, too."

"What are you talking about?"

She shook her head in bitter self-recrimination. "While our *intentions* might be good…in the end, a marriage born out of ease and convenience is never going to work over the long haul. Not for us, and certainly not for your girls or any other children we might have."

The heaviness of rejection sank in.

"So you won't even consider this?" he asked, wondering how his hopes and dreams could be any more destroyed. He paced closer, feeling more resentful with every second that passed. "You're still holding out for something better than what we have?" What he could give?

Her eyes darkened. "For all of our sakes, I have to, Jack."

Sorrow hit him harder than ever. "Well, in that case…" Slipping the jewelry box back in his pocket, he regarded her in bitter disappointment. "I think it's best that our relationship end."

Achingly aware the lifelong happiness he'd hoped to have with her was never going to materialize after all, he turned on his heel and walked out.

Chapter Sixteen

Jack ran into his mother in the hospital maternity ward the following day. She was standing on the other side of the glass, gazing raptly at her two new grandsons.

Wistfulness welling up inside him, he walked over to join her. Funny, just hours before, he had been hoping he and Bess would have their own baby born here. Now, the one time they had crossed paths while at the hospital, he to work, she to see her sister, she'd ducked her head, pretending she hadn't seen him, and had headed off the other way.

But that was beside the point. He had new family to welcome. "How are they doing?" he asked.

His mother flashed a joyous smile. "Beautifully."

The boys certainly looked as healthy as could be. Jack turned away from the glass. "Any idea when they'll be released from the hospital?" he asked casually.

"Hopefully, Christmas Eve. Bridgett wants to be

home when she and Cullen and Robby and Riot wake up on Christmas morning."

Made sense, Jack thought.

His mom touched his arm. "Speaking of holiday plans," she said. "Do you have a moment to talk privately?"

"Sure." Together, they went up to his office. Jack shut the door and gestured for Rachel to take a seat. He moved behind his desk. "So what's up?"

"That's what I wanted to ask you."

He lifted a brow.

"Bridgett just told me that Bess is no longer coming to the McCabe Christmas party with you and the girls on Christmas Eve." Rachel leaned forward. "Why is that?"

Jack scrubbed a hand over his face. "It's complicated, Mom."

"I understand complicated."

Jack was sure she did. "At the end of the day, I'm not going to be able to give Bess what she wants," he admitted wearily.

His mom's eyes darkened. "Which is?"

"The kind of all-out romantic love she has always wanted."

"You're saying you don't love her?" she asked in surprise.

Jack grimaced. "I do. You know that."

Rachel peered at him, considering. "But as a friend."

As so much more. Not that it seemed to matter. He stood and shoved his hands in his pockets. "I don't think she'd want the two of us discussing this, Mom. Any more than I want to be discussing it with you."

"I see. You think Bess would rather you keep everything you're thinking and feeling all bottled up inside?"

Jack swallowed around the knot in his throat. "She'd rather I were the kind of man she could fall head over heels in love with." Obviously, he wasn't.

"Ah." His mom nodded. "So, it's Bess who doesn't love *you*, the way *you* need."

His mother was making him sound selfish, when just the opposite was true. "Like I said, Mom…" Jack gave a disgruntled sigh. "…it's complicated."

Most of all, he wanted Bess to be happy. To have everything she had ever dreamed of.

Rachel stood, too. "So tell Bess what's in your heart. And uncomplicate it." She paused to let her words sink in, then went on, "We don't get very many chances to have all our dreams come true in this life. You and Bess both need to consider that before the two of you make an even bigger mistake."

Just before closing time that evening, Bess stopped by Monroe's Western Wear to pick up the special engraved collars and matching leashes for Princess Abigayle and Lady Grace. Nick had set them aside for her, as requested, when the package had arrived. She followed him into his private office.

Looking as incredibly happy as he had since his friendship with Sage Lockhart had segued into everlasting love, Nick said, "You know I would have dropped these off for you." He passed right by Bess's house when he drove home from work every evening.

"I know. I thought I would save you the trouble."

"Uh-huh." He studied her as if he was the older sibling instead of the baby of the family. "What's really going on?" He lifted the package off the shelf. "I stopped by the hospital this afternoon to see Bridgett and Cullen and the twins, and Bridgett said she thought you and Jack had some sort of falling-out."

"Not exactly."

"Really?" Edging closer, Nick regarded her with brotherly concern. "'Cause you look like you're feeling pretty blue. And with Christmas only a few days away? Definitely not a good sign."

As if she didn't know that. One minute she'd had it all. Or thought she did. Now...? "So I'm Grinchy." Doing her best to retain her composure, she ran her hand idly over the shipping label. "Like that's a big surprise."

"Actually—" Nick perched on the edge of his desk "—given the way you've been walking on air the past few weeks, it is. So what gives?"

Bess knew she had to talk to someone. If anyone in her family would understand, it would probably be the once way too driven but now happily married Nick. He had once risked everything and crashed and burned, too. "Jack knows I really want a baby and he offered to try to help me achieve that."

"As friends?"

She sat down in the chair in front of his desk and balanced the package on her knees. "We both agreed we'd have to get married if we went down that path. At least here in Laramie."

Nick braced his hands on either side of him. "But you don't want to get hitched strictly as a matter of convenience."

She lifted her shoulders in a listless shrug. "I would... if...there was even the possibility that he could ever love me the way a husband should love his wife. But..." Her voice cracked.

He handed her a tissue. "Did he say it wasn't a possibility?"

She wiped her eyes. "No. But he didn't offer any hope that we could ever be anything but lovers and friends, either. And..."

He sat back. "There's more?"

She blew her nose and did her best to pull herself together. "I think Jack might feel the tiniest bit sorry for me, or maybe just guilty because, as he said, for several years our relationship has been all about me giving and him taking."

Nick squinted. "You didn't get anything out of it?"

She leaped to her feet and began to pace. "Of course I did! I got to spend time with him and his three beautiful girls. When I was with them, it was as if I were part of their family," she said as the store intercom continued to play Christmas music.

"And then you became lovers."

"Hey." Bess spun around. "I never said that!"

He regarded her kindly. "Didn't have to. Everyone who looked at you together at the Monroe family get-together knew something had changed since Thanksgiving. Something pretty wonderful, if you ask me."

She had felt that way, too. Until Jack had delivered his incredibly lackluster proposal.

"But is it enough?" she asked, still aching over the unromantic hue of it all. She knew if anyone would understand, it would be Nick. With a confused shake of her head, she continued, "You and Sage began your relationship as lovers and friends. And *then* decided to marry and have a child together." And they were both so happy now.

Did that mean she and Jack had a chance, too?

"Actually, first we got pregnant. Deliberately," Nick

corrected, with a grin. "So Sage could have the baby she wanted. Then we got married."

"Still." Bess felt on the verge of tears again, struggling to find a way out of this mess she and Jack had made. "You and Sage weren't claiming to be madly in love then."

"Which was a mistake," he said. "Because we were in love with each other, Bess. From the very beginning. We were both just too wary of risking what we had as friends to take the giant leap of faith required to be that vulnerable and lay our hearts on the line. And our initial lack of complete candor almost cost us everything," he warned.

And yet, she thought, the former best friends turned lovers had found their way back to each other. And were happier than ever now.

Could that happen for her and Jack, as well?

Nick paused to study her. "I'm guessing you know how you feel?"

She nodded, as the reality of the situation came crashing back. Tears blurred her eyes. "The problem is, Jack's already had the love of *his* life."

"Doesn't mean he can't have another," he said sternly. He took both her hands in his. "Trust me on this, sis. There's no quota on love. Not for Jack. Not for you. Not for anyone."

Bess and Jack had agreed after their breakup that she would vacate the premises whenever he came over to visit with his puppy, in order to spare them any awkward encounters. The handoff late Christmas Eve was to be done similarly.

However, after two long, lonely days of having no contact with Jack except via text, she was ready to rethink that pact. As well as every other objection she'd had to their present and future arrangements.

Luckily, the text message she got from Jack the evening of December 23 told her he was feeling the same.

Coming over as soon as you give the go-ahead.

When I get there…can we talk?

Which was, as it turned out, exactly what she wanted to do. She just hadn't figured out when or how to approach him. Now she didn't have to.

Her heart filling with hope, Bess texted back, See you in twenty minutes. And yes, I'd love to talk. She followed that with a smiley face emoji, then rushed to get ready for his arrival.

Her pulse racing, she replaced her worn jeans and nursing school T-shirt with her favorite black skirt and a cranberry silk blouse. Brushed her teeth and styled her hair. Put on fresh makeup and a spritz of perfume. She was just trying to decide between ballet flats or heels when the doorbell rang.

She went for the heels.

Smoothing her skirt, she took a deep breath and went to open the door. Jack stood on the other side. Seeing him standing there, so strong and tall and handsome, so…*Jack*…melted her heart.

He seemed to have taken the same care getting ready for their meeting. Noting how closely he had shaved and how good he smelled, she ushered him inside.

He cast a fond glance at the two pups, who were sound asleep in their crates, then shrugged out of his coat and draped it over a wingback chair. The line of his mouth was sober as he turned to her, his eyes just as serious.

Bess's spirits rose and crashed and rose again. There was so much on the line.

Too much?

He strolled toward her, looking more coolly determined than she had ever seen him. The romantic, impetuous side of her wanted to throw herself into his arms then and there. However, her more practical side urged her to slow down and proceed more cautiously this time. They could get this right.

He cleared his throat and kept his eyes on hers. "Thanks for agreeing to be here when I came over to see the puppies."

She nodded. She wanted to start the reconciliation process by letting him know what was in her heart and understanding what was in his. She hitched in a shaky breath and spoke around the lump in her throat. "The truth is, I wanted to talk to you, too. First..." She edged closer and tilted her face up to his. "...I'm sorry about the way I reacted the other day."

His lips tightening with regret, he said, "You were right to shoot down my proposal. It was way too lame and spur of the moment."

The pain in his low tone matched the anguish she'd felt in her heart. Bess tensed. "Does this mean you're taking back your offer?"

"It means," he said, taking her hand and holding it between them, "I think we need to back up a little bit and consider where we are. And how we got to this point in our relationship in the first place." He released a rough breath. "I never meant to hurt you, Bess."

"I never meant to hurt you, either."

Sorrow tugged at the ruggedly handsome planes of his face. "Yet we have hurt each other."

She nodded. If they were going to move forward in

the way she wanted, they were going to have to bare their souls, difficult as it might be. With a sigh of regret, she led him over to sit down on the sofa. "Part of it is because I've had conditions all along."

He settled next to her, his broad shoulders straining the cashmere of his pine-green sweater. "In what sense?"

Bess turned toward him, keeping her hand clasped in his. Where to begin?

"Well, at first, I thought I could spend time with you, as long as we remained just friends. Then," she admitted ruefully, "it was going to be okay to want more than that from you, as long as we were lovers only once, and then when that did not seem at all sufficient, just for the Christmas holidays."

He grinned, clearly recalling just how irrevocably passionate they had been.

"And when that still wasn't enough," she continued, "I decided I could be your friend and lover and maybe… *if* things worked out the way I hoped…even marry you and have a baby with you one day." She shook her head, reflecting unhappily, "But I only wanted to do that if I were the new love of your life. I didn't want to just be a placeholder or some kind of convenient substitute for the wife you lost."

He looked at her with a quiet understanding that brought forth a spate of feelings. "But now your feelings have changed," he said, as if seeking to understand.

She tightened her fingers in his, at long last ready to put it all on the line. "I had a heart-to-heart with Nick. He told me there are no quotas on love. That just because you loved Gayle with all your heart and soul did not mean that you couldn't love me that way, too. And…" She drew a bolstering breath and looked deep into his eyes. "…after I thought about it, I realized that there are no conditions on love. If you want it to bloom, then you have to accept it and be open to it and let it grow in its own way and its own time. There are no arbitrary limits or conditions. I realize that now."

He used his thumb to wipe away the tears trembling on her lower lashes. "You aren't the only one who has made mistakes," he said, shifting her onto his lap. "I've been trying to play it safe in every way possible since Gayle died. I thought if I shut down that part of my heart that I could protect the happiness and good fortune I still had left. Keep myself and my children from being hurt."

She understood that.

"Part of that meant not letting myself get involved with you as anything more than a casual friend, and that worked, for a while."

"For both of us," she agreed, acutely aware of the mistakes they had made.

"But then, as my grief faded, and I started to come back to life, I became more and more aware of you. As a woman and as a potential love interest."

Bess tilted her head. Seeing the desire in his eyes, she felt a shiver deep inside her. "Which is why, I'm guessing, you were so unhappy about me going out on a date with Tim Briscoe."

The crinkles around his eyes deepened. "I tried to be decent about it. Support whatever it was that you desired. I really wanted you to be happy."

She chuckled at the twinkle in his cobalt blue eyes. "But…?"

"The truth was, if you were going to date anyone," he admitted, "I wanted it to be me. And only me."

She smiled. "Why didn't you tell me that was how you felt?"

"Because I'm a McCabe."

And hence brought up to be gallant to the core, she realized.

His voice dropped a sexy notch. "I knew back then how you felt about jumping into another romance with someone who was on the rebound, and that caution went double for someone who'd already had it all. I cared about you too much to hurt you that way." His gaze devoured her, head to toe, and he stroked the inside of her wrist with the pad of his thumb. "I wanted you to have everything you deserved, including a baby and a larger-than-life love. And since you apparently saw me as just a pal—" he exhaled in apparent frustration "—I didn't want to do anything to ruin our friendship."

"Nor did I." Bess splayed her hands over his chest; the rapid beat of his heart matched hers. "Which was why I was trying so hard to move on and date someone else. I was trying to get over wanting you."

He threaded a hand through her hair, wrapped the other around her waist. "But it didn't work with Tim."

Emotion welled within her. "The whole time I was out on that date with him, I felt like I was cheating on you."

"Unwarranted," he pointed out, "since technically we didn't have anything other than friendship at that point."

She snuggled against him, taking all the heat and strength he had to give. "The frustrating thing was, I really wanted it to be different between you and me, even then. I just didn't know how to go about it."

He drew a deep breath, his eyes never leaving hers. Letting her know she wasn't the only one who had been doing an incredible amount of soul-searching. "Hence, the cranky versus fake-happy Christmas letters."

· Grinning, she lamented, "I had to get all that emotion out somewhere."

He stroked his palm lovingly over her spine. "When I read them, I figured you were in trouble."

No kidding. She'd been headed for the most miserable holiday season ever. "Which was why you promptly rode in to my rescue," she said with relief.

"I just didn't have any idea at that point your angst had anything to do with me." He lifted her hand to his mouth and kissed the back of her knuckles.

"Well, it did."

They exchanged smiles. Jack shifted her off his lap and stood, drawing her to her feet. He pulled her against him, so they were touching in one long, sexy line. "You know what the most ironic thing of all this is, darlin'?" He left a trail of kisses down her neck that set off a firestorm of heat. "While you were lusting after marriage and a baby…"

And he'd been saying *never again…*

He drew back to look into her eyes. "Little by little, I secretly found myself wanting those things again, too. But not with just anyone. I wanted to have it all with you," he said in that tender-rough voice she adored. "Because I love you, Bess, and I have for a long time now."

Happiness swept through her in waves. "Oh, Jack," she whispered. "I love you, too."

She closed her eyes and his lips moved over hers, sweetly, evocatively.

"Enough to give me another chance to give you the kind of all-out, romantic courtship you deserve?" he asked, his voice filled with all the love he felt for her.

Tired of downplaying her own wishes, Bess gathered all her courage and corrected, "Enough to stop playing the waiting game. Or pretend we have to do things in any particular time frame or any set way. I love you enough to marry you, just the way you wanted, and become a mother to your three girls and owner to two adorable golden retriever puppies."

"As well as have our baby."

At last. The heartfelt proposal she had been waiting for all her life. Bess nodded. "Whenever we both decide the time is right."

"You mean that," he noted in wonder.

She drew another tremulous breath. "With all my heart and soul, Doc." She rose on tiptoe and sealed her promise with another kiss.

When they finally drew apart, she said, "In the meantime, I have a little something for you." She went to get a small wrapped gift from beneath her tabletop tree.

He opened it. Inside the box was an old-fashioned pocket watch. "It's beautiful."

She turned it over, so he could see the back. Engraved into the gold was a pair of angel wings. "I got the idea when we were watching *It's a Wonderful Life*. I realized that night you were *my* guardian angel. And I wanted it to continue."

"For all time?"

"Well, Doc, that was the hope."

Jack grinned. "I love it. And just so you know—" he waggled his brows in a way that engendered a wealth of anticipation "—I have a little something for you, too." From his pocket, he pulled out the small dark blue jeweler's box he'd brought with him the day of their breakup. The box she had never accepted.

"You kept it," she marveled.

"Hope springs eternal, and all that. Of course I kept it." He gave her a mock indignant look, then encouraged, "Open it. See what's inside."

"Oh, Jack." She caught her breath at the sheer beauty of the gift. "An infinity necklace!" Made out of solid gold, the chain held two never-ending loops with a diamond-studded heart caught in between. The heart was engraved. Tears of happiness blurring her eyes, she read aloud, "'Forever yours. Love, Jack.'" Her hands trembling, she caught it to her chest. "It's perfect!"

He moved behind her to put it on, nuzzling her neck in the process. "As are you."

After they'd admired it in the mirror, she turned back to face him. "So, what next?"

He bent to kiss her, thoroughly and passionately. "Well, darlin', since you asked, I'm up for a little holiday romance."

She laughed. A lifetime of joy swept through her. She kissed him again and then drawled, "Well, what do you know, Doc. I'm up for some, too."

He guided her beneath the mistletoe she had hung, just in case. Their adorable puppies slept on.

"Merry Christmas, darlin'," Jack whispered happily.

Bess wreathed her arms about his neck and guided him wonderfully close, knowing at long last all her dreams had come true. She fitted her lips to his and kissed him. "Merry Christmas to you, too."

Epilogue

December 1, two years later

Jack joined Bess in the living room after all five of their children were snuggled in their beds, sound asleep. A cozy fire blazed in the hearth, beneath a row of colorful Christmas stockings strung across the mantel. The tree was lit, with their children's artwork and an assortment of colorful decorations taking center stage. But it was his lovely wife who captivated him the most.

He stood for a moment, taking her in. In a red sweater and trim black skirt, her spectacular legs cloaked by matching tights, she was as gorgeous as ever.

His heart swelling with love, he strolled toward her. "Did you get your Christmas letter done yet?"

Bess motioned for him to take a place beside her on the sofa. As he sank down beside her, she showed him her handiwork. "Almost."

He breathed in her sweet feminine scent, as he leaned in to study the handwritten note. He pressed a cheek to her temple. "Was it hard to compose?"

She bussed his jawline, then drew back far enough to smile at him provocatively. "Only in the sense that I didn't want to go on ad nauseam."

He chuckled, knowing exactly what she meant. They were living an enviably happy life these days. He wrapped his arm around her shoulders and guessed, "But you did have a lot of good things to report."

"Oh, yes." She set her letter aside and shifted over onto his lap. Then, settling her arms around him, she gazed into his eyes. "Starting with the fact that our two six-month-old sons are the spitting image of their very handsome daddy."

It was hard to believe they now had two boys and three girls.

She stroked her thumb across his cheek. "And their three older sisters love entertaining them."

He turned his head and kissed the back of her hand. They exchanged smiles. Another wave of joy swept through him as he wrapped a wayward lock of her silky hair around his fingertip. "As do we and the beloved Mrs. D."

Bess mugged playfully. "What would we do without her?"

She was definitely a member of their family. "Not sure either of us ever want to find out." Although once again, Mrs. D. had cut back on her hours just a little bit and only worked days now. Which gave Jack and Bess all the privacy they needed during the evenings.

He murmured, "Seriously, it has been a very good year."

"A very good *two* years," Bess corrected.

During that time, they'd married. She'd sold her home at a tidy little profit. And like her twin sister, she had delivered twin boys.

"Indeed."

She gazed over at their two golden retrievers. They were grown dogs now, and as loving and gentle spirited as they were playful. "Lady Grace and Princess Abigayle would certainly agree, too." Exhausted by an afternoon of playing with the kids, the two pets snuggled side by side in their cushioned dog beds.

Jack nodded at the nearly finished Christmas letter. "I hope you told everyone that our two golden retrievers were the stars of their obedience class."

"I might have mentioned that, too," she teased. "Along with the fact that Chloe, Nicole and Lindsay remain convinced that it was really Santa who engineered the advent of their new mommy, two puppies and two baby brothers." She cupped his face in her hands and kissed him sweetly.

His heart filling, he gathered her closer and kissed her back, just as tenderly. "If you think about it, given where we both were a little over two years ago, it kind of does all sound magical…"

She splayed her hands across his chest. "It feels that way, too," she murmured contentedly.

They ruminated about their good fortune, all the love they had ever wanted flowing between them. Knowing all their dreams had definitely come true, he kissed her again, then said, "So, Mrs. McCabe, was it a glass-half-full or glass-half-empty kind of year?"

Bess's eyes glittered with happiness. "With you, Dr. McCabe? And our very merry crew? It will always and forever be a glass *overflowing* kind of life." She kissed him ardently this time. "Merry Christmas, sweetheart."

Jack returned the sweet caress with all the love and passion he had to give. "Merry Christmas to you, too."

* * * * *

WE HOPE YOU ENJOYED THIS BOOK!

HARLEQUIN®

SPECIAL EDITION

Open your heart to more true-to-life stories of love and family.

Discover six new books available every month, wherever books are sold.

AVAILABLE THIS MONTH FROM
Harlequin® Special Edition

THE RIGHT REASON TO MARRY
The Bravos of Valentine Bay • by Christine Rimmer

Unexpected fatherhood changes everything for charming bachelor Liam Bravo. He wants to marry Karin Killigan, the mother of his child. But Karin won't settle for less than lasting true love.

MAVERICK CHRISTMAS SURPRISE
Montana Mavericks: Six Brides for Six Brothers
by Brenda Harlen

Rancher Wilder Crawford is in no hurry to get married and start a family—until a four-month-old baby is left on his doorstep on Christmas Day!

THE RANCHER'S BEST GIFT
Men of the West • by Stella Bagwell

Rancher Matthew Waggoner was planning to be in and out of Red Bluff as quickly as possible. But staying with his boss's sister, Camille Hollister, proves to be more enticing than he thought. Will these two opposites be able to work through their differences and get the best Christmas gift?

IT STARTED AT CHRISTMAS...
Gallant Lake Stories • by Jo McNally

Despite lying on her résumé, Amanda Lowery still manages to land a job designing Halcyon House for Blake Randall—and a place to stay over Christmas. Neither of them have had much to celebrate, but with Blake's grieving nephew staying at Halcyon, they're all hoping for some Christmas magic.

A TALE OF TWO CHRISTMAS LETTERS
Texas Legends: The McCabes • by Cathy Gillen Thacker

Rehab nurse Bess Monroe is mortified that she accidentally sent out two Christmas letters—one telling the world about her lonely life instead of the positive spin she wanted! And when Jack McCabe, widowed surgeon and father of three, sees the second one, he offers his friendship to get through the holidays. But their pact soon turns into something more...

THE SOLDIER'S SECRET SON
The Culhanes of Cedar River • by Helen Lacey

When Jake Culhane comes home to Cedar River, he doesn't expect to reconnect with the woman he never forgot. Abby Perkins is still in love with the boy who broke her heart when he enlisted. This could be their first Christmas as a real family—if Abby can find the courage to tell Jake the truth.

LOOK FOR THESE AND OTHER HARLEQUIN SPECIAL EDITION BOOKS WHEREVER BOOKS ARE SOLD, INCLUDING MOST BOOKSTORES, SUPERMARKETS, DISCOUNT STORES AND DRUGSTORES.

HSEATMBPA1219

COMING NEXT MONTH FROM

⬧H HARLEQUIN®

SPECIAL EDITION

Available December 17, 2019

#2737 FORTUNE'S FRESH START
The Fortunes of Texas: Rambling Rose • by Michelle Major
In the small Texas burg of Rambling Rose, real estate investor Callum Fortune is making a big splash. The last thing he needs is any personal complications slowing his pace—least of all nurse Becky Averill, a beautiful widow with twin baby girls!

#2738 HER RIGHT-HAND COWBOY
Forever, Texas • by Marie Ferrarella
A clause in her father's will requires Ena O'Rourke to work the family ranch for six months before she can sell it. She's livid at her father throwing a wrench in her life from beyond the grave. But Mitch Randall, foreman of the Double E, is always there for her. As Ena spends more time on the ranch—and with Mitch—new memories are laid over the old...and perhaps new opportunities to make a life.

#2739 SECOND-CHANCE SWEET SHOP
Wickham Falls Weddings • by Rochelle Alers
Brand-new bakery owner Sasha Manning didn't anticipate that the teenager she hired would have a father more delectable than anything in her shop window! Sasha still smarts from falling for a man too good to be true. Divorced single dad Dwight Adams will have to prove to Sasha that he's the real deal and not a wolf in sheep's clothing...and learn to trust someone with his heart along the way.

#2740 COOKING UP ROMANCE
The Taylor Triplets • by Lynne Marshall
Lacy was a redhead with a pink food truck who prepared mouthwatering meals. Hunky construction manager Zack Gardner agreed to let her feed his hungry crew in exchange for cooking lessons for his young daughter. But it looked like the lovely businesswoman was transforming the single dad's life in more ways than one—since a family secret is going to change both of their lives in ways they never expected.

#2741 RELUCTANT HOMETOWN HERO
Wildfire Ridge • by Heatherly Bell
Former army officer Ryan Davis doesn't relish the high-profile role of town sheriff, but when duty calls, he responds. Even if it means helping animal rescuer Zoey Castillo find her missing foster dog. When Ryan asks her out, Zoey is wary of a relationship in the spotlight—especially given her past. If the sheriff wants to date her, he'll have to prove that two legs are better than four.

#2742 THE WEDDING TRUCE
Something True • by Kerri Carpenter
For the sake of their best friends' wedding, divorce attorney Xander Ryan and wedding planner Grace Harris are calling a truce. Now they must plan the perfect wedding shower together. But Xander doesn't believe in marriage! And Grace believes in romance and true love. Clearly, they have nothing in common. In fact, all Xander feels when Grace is near is disdain and...desire. Wait. What?

HSECNM1219